*A*
*Harlequin*
*Romance*

# SEVEN OF MAGPIES

*by*

## DORIS E. SMITH

**HARLEQUIN** **BOOKS**

Winnipeg • Canada          New York • New York

SEVEN OF MAGPIES

First published in 1970 by Mills & Boon Limited,
17 - 19 Foley Street, London, England.

Harlequin Canadian edition published December, 1970
Harlequin U.S. edition published March, 1971

*All the characters in this book have no existence outside the imagination
of the Author, and have no relation whatsoever to anyone bearing the
same name or names. They are not even distantly inspired by any individual known or unknown to the Author, and all the incidents are pure
invention.*

# CHAPTER ONE

COACH tours up the Norfolk coast neglected no item in interest—the tall tower of Winterton church, the beautifully restored Horsey windmill and the red and white Happisborough lighthouse. Nearby was a "pull-in" for refreshments, and some years ago alighting passengers often met another interesting phenomenon—Johanna Dykes, aged five, wheeling her doll's pram along the road from her father's farm.

"Is that your dolly, dear?" they would ask of the toffee brown fringe and the solemn eyes.

The reply was startling. "No. It's my little sister," and the enquirers, peering down, would see a plump tabby kitten. "Isn't she *very* like me?" Johanna would flute, and the addressees, mesmerized by two pairs of questioning eyes and two baby mouths, each shaped like a circumflex accent, would find themselves agreeing.

"Binkie's the one with the tail!" the small voice would add.

That had been fifteen years ago, but it was extraordinary how ever since Saturday, when she'd come home from college, the ghost of that much petted little girl had been everywhere. Now from the window of her bedroom, high up under the terracotta roof of the old farmhouse, Johanna could almost see the white-socked child that had been herself running over the fields that still stretched green upon green, as she'd thought then, to the end of the world.

Against the window Dorothy Dykes, her mother, was at this moment leaning. She had come up to watch Johanna pack, had even offered lightheartedly to do it for her. The offer having been declined, she was now craning her slim neck upwards, and next moment—

"Mummy, what *are* you doing?" Johanna asked, staring as her parent hitched herself on to the window sill and hung perilously outwards, hands and forearms berry brown against the rolled-up sleeves of her pale blue gingham shirt.

"One, two, three, four, five, six—*seven*!" Her mother's

5

ruffled head came back into the bedroom. "Is it yours, darling? Have *you* got a secret?"

All of a sudden the room felt icy cold and still.

"Secret?" Johanna stammered, and moistened her dry lips. She'd been walking the tightrope since Saturday, relaxing just that little bit more each day until now, Tuesday afternoon, with less than an hour before she would be away from Dykes Lynn and heading for Scotland.

"*Jo! Darling!*" Her mother was looking at her with wrinkled brow. "You went quite green. Do you feel all right?"

"Not when you do things like that!" she cornered. "Honestly, Mum, if that had been me you'd have looked green too! All forty shades of it!" And caught her breath. Ireland—Donegal—it was perilous ground.

Her mother, however, was laughing. "Phooey! Come here and meet my family. I've had my eye on father and mother since March, but I only saw the children a week ago, and then they weren't all together so I wasn't sure. But now, just look!"

Obediently Johanna craned upwards to the azure sky and the television aerial. Posed on it were two large and five small magpies, streamlined and motionless as jets on the tarmac. And yet for a second the white and blue-black plumage and the long down-folded tails appeared to gyrate.

"*Seven for a secret that shall never be told.*"

But you *will* tell, she reminded herself, as soon as it's over . . . Myles will help.

"They're lovely," she rejoined dully, and withdrew her head, disconcerted to find her mother's gaze still on her.

"Jo, forgive me, darling, but—there *is* something wrong!"

"No, Mum," said Johanna, picking up a sweater. "Nothing. Honestly."

It worked. One further second of hesitation and then her mother was on her feet. "Right, then. I'll go and round up your transport."

And that's the way you want it, Johanna said fiercely to the spineless thing inside her that had suddenly almost craved to be bullied into confession.

"Don't be too long, darling. The train is five to," her

6

mother, herself notoriously unpunctual, abjured her from the doorway.

"No, I'm just ready." Sponge bag? Yes. Hairbrush? On the dressing table.

The dressing table had deep yellow skirts and a square triple mirror in a white frame. It had thrown back plaits and gym tunic, ponytail and sweater. To-day it showed a caramel white-piped dress and a small cropped head, nut brown. "Like a blooming bit of mahogany," Myles had said once. "How are things in Polonesia?" was another of his salutations.

At first he had refused completely to believe that she'd been born and bred on a Norfolk farm. His own roots were in Donegal and he looked like it—over six foot of lean long leg and wide shoulder, and the clefted chin that went with tweed and collies. Except that these days Myles had no connection with collies. Tweed, yes. He and Johanna were studying textile design at the same School of Art in London, with the difference that, while Johanna had now just sat for her final examinations, Myles had come from Dublin only seven weeks ago to do a special course for mature students.

He had Irish eyes, bold and turquoisy, and they never stopped smiling, not even when he wrote off his car round a traffic bollard or was bawled out for perching Johanna on a turret tank in a battle area to take her photograph. That had been the weekend she'd brought him home, but thank heaven the incident had not got to her father's ears. He would certainly have reacted exactly as the commandant who had evicted them. As it was, the hot angry fragments into which that weekend had exploded were agony enough to remember.

Seeing Myles off and coming in bubbling with happiness to tell her news. Permission had seemed a foregone conclusion. It wasn't. Her father: "Only one word for it— preposterous! And what's he leaving this to you for? Too much sense to face me himself?" Her mother cutting in as she'd tried to explain that telling them alone had been her idea: "But, darling, how long have you known him?" Her father exploding again: "Four *weeks*! And he's got the nerve to . . ." Sharply, his tone had changed. "There's nothing else we should know about, is there?"

7

Afterwards, more quietly, it had boiled down to "talking about it again in a year's time", with a footnote from her mother: "Don't look like that, Jo. It's not for ever. Just till you know each other a bit longer. Myles will understand, he's a nice boy." Something, at least, to fasten on. They did like Myles (who could help it?).

Her mother's voice sounded: "Jo! It's gone five past, dear!"

"Beginnings don't matter," she said defiantly to the girl in the white-framed mirror, turned, grabbed the suitcase and ran downstairs.

May had been hot, June had come in hotter still. Johanna's father in shirt-sleeves was polishing dead flies off the windscreen in preparation for the drive to Great Yarmouth where Johanna was catching a train. It would have been nearly as short to drive direct to Norwich, but there were reasons for Great Yarmouth, reasons which had to do with the new suit Edward had come home with yesterday, and the fact that its trousers were generously cut. One look and Dorothy had declared that he must take it back. She was now saying in honeyed tones: "You forgot something, dear," and leaning into the station wagon to place an oblong box on the back seat.

"Okay, ready!" Johanna called a little breathlessly, and went forward.

"Have a lovely time, darling," her mother bade, kissing her. "You've earned it after all the hard work. And don't forget to give my love to Sue."

"No, of course not." What would they say when they knew that she hadn't gone near Sue? Scotland yes, Sue in Peebles no. However, to begin with, the postcards would keep them from guessing. Views of Edinburgh and something like: "Here for the day."

"What about your results? Sure you don't want me to send them on?"

To Sue's house? She shivered. Myles hadn't told her how to get out of this one. "Quite sure, thanks. If I've done badly I don't want to know about it on holiday."

"Of course you haven't," her mother scoffed tenderly. "You'll have done splendidly, the way you always do."

Mile by mile, the home ground slipped away, the level new green of her father's peas, beans and potatoes, a

8

neighbour's field neatly dotted with hay bales, the ruins of an eleventh-century abbey, and on the left, far out and running with them, the thirty-foot coast wall that held back the greedy waters of the North Sea.

The road struck inland—Potter Heigham with cabin cruisers nudging each other in the cut, Catfield and Caister with its holiday camps, open but not yet in their fullest swing. At this point back to the coast again and along the North Denes to Great Yarmouth. The North Sea can be very grey and choppy, this afternoon it was a cool silvery blue.

"Nice place, Yarmouth," her father startled her by the observation. He had been a silent companion for several miles. "You could do worse than apply to them."

She'd almost forgotten. Her mother telling her about the teaching post which would become vacant there at the end of the month had done so with such typical non-involvement. "Just a thought, dear, you'll probably want to go much farther afield."

"If you got a little car you could live at home," her father was continuing, and added repetitiously, "Always been very fond of Yarmouth. You used to be too."

"I still am very fond of it," she answered truthfully— if you loved life at all you couldn't fail to be drawn to this lively, happy place. "But I don't think they'd want to appoint me for less than a year." It was a test statement even though a wretchedly unfair one. She would be twenty-one in the spring.

Her father's silence showed that he'd got the message— like a douche of cold water. He was a man who hated trouble, making it or meeting it, and he was a lot better at doing the latter.

She said impulsively: "Dad, I'm sorry, but you do realize I'm going to marry Myles?"

Now he was looking at her. He had blue eyes, kind, serious, cobalty, an English blue. "Well, you've been straight about it, Jo, I'll say that for you, and you've a right to your own mind, I respect that. I'll say another thing for you too." He glimpsed her suddenly stricken expression. "Hold hard, love, no need to look like that. I'm pleased with you. Reckon I'm not much good at making speeches, but I know you thought pretty badly

9

of me three weeks back and for all that you accepted what I said. Another girl might have gone off and done some tomfool thing she'd regret for the rest of her life."

Oh no! Johanna thought, not this, *please* . . .

"If I were to do that with Myles," she swallowed, "I wouldn't regret it."

This time, blessedly, the blue eyes remained fixed on the traffic bound for the market. "Or Myles?" their owner asked casually. Johanna gasped. "It takes two, you know," her father stated. "And it has to last a lifetime."

Speech returned. "Yes, Dad, I do know."

"Then give it a fair start, love. That's only sense. Your mother and I were engaged for just on two years."

"I know that too, Dad," she said gently. "*And* it didn't make any difference. You were sure from the beginning, too."

A smile broke over the blunt very English features. "All right, Jo, I reckon you've got me. If you know one another as you really are without any fancy stuff and still want to spend the rest of your lives together, that's good enough for me. And when the time comes . . ." Evidently he was not going to give in all the way. "You might think of having the wedding over there." Placidly he jerked his head towards the south front of St. Nicholas's Church.

"Why there, Dad?" she asked, staring at the pinnacled tower and the transept that had the window with the birds and the boats.

"Just thought you might like it," he answered gruffly. "It was where your mother and I wanted to get married. Unfortunately Hitler beat us to it."

"I don't know, Dad. I'll think about it. But after all, you and Mum got on all right." She spoke as the twenty-three notes from Bach's B Minor Mass sounded across Church Plain. It was quarter to three. Her father, with an exclamation, turned swiftly up The Conge and two minutes later the car had mounted the ramp, bumped gently over the bridge and pulled up.

"Eh, are you taking up your abode with Sue permanently?" her father joked, lifting the cases. Her heart missed a beat and subsided as he went on: "Should know

10

by this time, I suppose. Your mother packs a blinking trunk every time she goes on holiday too."

And she herself ought also to know by this time, Jo thought, smiling hurtfully. He was the last person to suspect or challenge. He took for granted that she would tell the truth.

A last slow question at the train. "By the way, where *is* Myles?"

"Oh!" Again she started foolishly. "At home." True at the moment. Myles was in Dublin, would be until this evening. Take-off time for his plane was seven.

"I suppose you'll be writing to him now and then." Another joke. She smiled mechanically. "Tell him to come and see us again soon."

She nodded, feeling the blood course through her cheeks. Embarking on this, she had been prepared for anything, anything except kindness and affection. Should she, late as it was . . .

"Watch out, Jo!" Her father's arm swept her out of the path of another traveller, a girl about her own age, holding by the hand a curly-haired sprite of African childhood in a red anorak.

The sprite, hugging a huge toy panda, had no free hand for the ascent into the train. She lifted a white sandal doubtfully and put it down again. Promptly, Edward Dykes stepped forward and swung her up the step. Smiles and "Thank yous" passed and during them the guard's whistle blew.

A tobacco-flavoured kiss landed on Johanna's cheek. "Nice little thing," her father said approvingly, and closed the carriage door.

A minute later the train chugged unconcernedly out of Yarmouth Vauxhall. It had thirty-five minutes to get to Norwich and it was not at all bothered. *Plenty of time, plenty of time,* it hissed comfortably, *seven for a secret, plenty of time.*

*Plenty of time, plenty of time* . . . But there hadn't been time enough. What with the clock chimes and the little girl, there had been no time in the end. In a matter of hours now she would be with Myles, in a matter of weeks his wife.

11

The wheel tune changed . . . *"Why did I choose you? Why did I choose you?* and she laughed to herself. In a way she hadn't chosen at all, Myles had just moved in. "Talk about a takeover," the others had said, and now the train was saying something else. *Yes, I do know. Yes, I do know.* Something she wouldn't tell a soul because they'd think badly of Myles, and even that panic-stricken moment had come because of love. She'd said so tremblingly, terrified in case she might lose him. "Right, then. Let's *get* married," Myles had said gaily. "What's stopping us?" It seemed only her parents. His knew nothing about it. They wouldn't object, Myles assured her, but of course they couldn't be told now because it would implicate them in the deception. The answer, he'd continued, was Scotland where, provided you could give proof of residence for the prescribed time, parental consent after the age of sixteen was unnecessary. Silly really to have gone home at all. Myles had wanted them to travel together last Friday when term had ended, but she couldn't, not without saying good-bye. Amenable as always, he'd fallen into line, even decided to follow her example and have the weekend at home.

She knew Myles was twenty-two and had an older brother, Douglas, and no sisters. His parents were tweed manufacturers, originally from Donegal but now living in Dublin—O'Malley Tweeds Ltd.—and Myles had gone into the business. That he was a live wire in it, she also knew, for though his present course of study had to do with styling and design, he was also, it seemed, Sales Organizer and Public Relations Officer. "He'll be a director, I suppose?" her father had hazarded, but that she did not know. Douglas O'Malley was one but seemed far less involved than Myles. "Doug can move when he wants to, otherwise he's not pushed. Never was the showy type," Myles had said with actually a note of affection. So that was another thing she knew. He was generous even towards the brother who didn't pull his weight.

The African child, her teeth showing like tiny pearls, had launched into song. "Pwaise Him, pwaise Him, all ye little children."

"Hush, Jill darling, we can't sing here," her companion looked apologetically at Johanna.

"Please don't stop her. I like it," Johanna said quickly.

The singer had the gifts of her race, unselfconsciousness, gaiety and sincerity. Dad would have enjoyed this, Johanna thought, and for no logical reason the memory of his big tweed-clad person and Jill's stick-like legs brought a lump to her throat. Her father had a weakness for little children. When she'd been that age he'd taken her for a walk every Sunday, lifting her over the rough ground and holding her up to sit on the pony. Dad would be tickled to have grandchildren, but would Myles want a family? They had never discussed it.

Love is what counts, Johanna argued, and Myles loves me. But there was still a niggle. "Right then, let's *get* married," suddenly seemed a bit glib and no firm plans had been made for the future. "Is it hard to get a flat in Dublin?" she had asked once. "Don't know. Shouldn't think so," Myles had answered easily, letting his fingers play on her arm. "We probably won't need one. There's bags of room at home." And when she'd demurred he'd said just as easily, "All right then. We'll *have* a flat. Anything you say."

First things first, Johanna reminded herself, and first things were a man and a woman loving each other, not a woman looking out for a home and babies. And yet would it last, that kind of loving?

This stage of the journey was nearly over. Two white sails showing across the green plain gave just the effect of one of her artist mother's paintings; nearer the train, wake bubbled from a cruiser speeding down the broad, and next came the boat yard full of painted hulls. Two minutes or so to Norwich and she was still in turmoil.

She thought it would be all right, she was almost sure of it, but not quite . . . she needed more time.

At that moment the name-boards "Norwich Thorpe" rushed past the window.

The girl in charge of "Jill" was coaxing the latter's spindly arms into the anorak. She smiled over at Johanna: "Well, here's where we leave you. I daresay you won't be sorry!" She was, Johanna had decided, either the child's housemother or teacher.

"We're getting off," "Jill" informed her brightly.

Sometimes it is the simplest movements that pull the

trigger. In this case it was the dark curly head bobbing towards the door.

Suddenly for Johanna time and speed were the only considerations. She was on her feet, she was standing on the seat tugging at the cases in the rack, and then she was hopping to the floor. The mirror caught her for a second, round-necked caramel dress, nut-brown boyish head, soft pink baby mouth, and lost her as she bumped the cases through the narrow door of the carriage.

The box clock at the end of the platform read: "The time now is 15.40." Myles was not checking in at Dublin Airport until half past six. There was ample time—but how to say it? How even to begin? "Darling, it's not that I don't love you . . ." "Darling, instead of Edinburgh could you come back here? I've got to talk to you." He'd be justifiably put out. He'd mapped the journey for her, a long one with several connections. He would feel that if he hadn't given in to her whim about going home she wouldn't have had the chance to back down.

She hated herself, and even the public address system now wafting across the station seemed to have a reproachful note.

"The train now standing at platform three is the fifteen-forty-five for Lincoln . . ."

At the barrier the ticket collector frowned at what she had handed him. "Edinburgh? You want the Lincoln train, miss. You've just got off it."

"I know," she stammered. "I know. I've changed my mind."

Jill and her custodian were standing at the bookstall. She passed them, conscious of the latter's surprised look, found a phone booth and dragged her cases inside. It seemed significant that as she dialled the public address sounded again, muffled but audible.

"The train now leaving platform three is the fifteen-forty-five for Lincoln calling at Thetford, Ely, March, Spalding and Sleaford."

The line was clear, the delay fractional. At the other end a male voice answered. "Myles?" Johanna asked eagerly.

There was an intake of breath, sharp, immediate and apparently all. Something about the silence sent her heart

14

into her throat. "Please," she said breathlessly. "Please could I speak to Mr. Myles O'Malley?"

This time the voice did reply. "Oh, lord!" it said with an Irish accent. "Haven't you heard?"

"Heard what?" she faltered. It was hard to speak against the battering in her chest.

The voice went cagey. "Look, are you a friend of his?"

Johanna had thought that both her heart and brain had turned to blocks of ice, but yet signals were getting in. *Remember they don't know—anything—wait till you talk to Myles.* "Not really," she said. "Has—something happened?"

"Yes. That's why I didn't want to give you too much of a shock," the other voice returned. "He bought it yesterday—driving up to Belfast on his way to Larne. He was going over from there to Stranraer to meet some guy he was going touring with in Scotland."

"Bought it?" Johanna moistened her lips. "You mean —is he badly hurt?"

"More than that, I'm afraid," her informant answered. "He's dead."

The young housemother, taking Jill to the Ladies, was the first to notice the half open door of the telephone booth and to glance casually inside. Johanna lying limply across her cases saw nothing. She heard nothing either, for all that the telephone was still clasped in her hand.

## CHAPTER TWO

"So I thought tomorrow we'd have lunch in Town and go to this exhibition," Jessie Lee's voice tailed off and she gazed compassionately at her young guest. The child had such a "little boy" look . . . a Babe in the Wood steeling his coral pink lip, round brown pupils under a pudding-basin haircut. And yet heart-rendingly feminine.

Johanna's mother, Dorothy Dykes, an old school friend, had warned her not to ask questions. "She won't talk about it. She's hardly told us a thing, just that she tried to phone Myles from Norwich, some little thing she wanted to say to him, I don't know what, and they told

15

her there'd been this accident. And then it was all so odd really. She wouldn't let me ring the friend she was going to stay with in Scotland, insisted on doing it herself, and now for some reason she won't hear of going there. And the doctor does want her to get away."

"She could always come here, you know that," Jessie had said. "Only I don't suppose Wimbledon is much of a change."

But, touchingly, Johanna had come, and over supper had been making a gallant show of interest in the latest about Jessie's family, her son Alan in Nairobi and her daughter Deborah, the Home Economics teacher, who had made news last November by marrying Colin Cameron the singer.

It was beginning again and it would go on and on, round and round into that dreadful whirlpool—if you'd really loved him, if you'd said yes, *how* wrong? Such a little wrong compared with what happened . . . he *died* . . . because you said you'd have to be married . . . and because you had to go home . . . and then you weren't sure . . .

"I'm terribly sorry, Mrs. Lee. What were you saying?"

Jessie explained about the exhibition of fabrics in the Irish exhibition centre in the West End, a specialized showing and not for the general public, but John knew someone who knew someone else in the Irish Export Board and he'd got them an invitation. She stopped short, looking aghast. "Oh, my dear, I didn't think—perhaps you wouldn't like it . . ." Clearly she was thinking that Myles had been in the same line and, moreover, had been Irish. Johanna was thinking that too. Well, you couldn't go through life running away. "Of course I'd like it," she said firmly. "Very much indeed."

"See she gets there, Jo. That chap will be looking out for you," John Lee had said at breakfast, and after a few hours of Jessie in London, Johanna's dread of the associations Donegal tweed would bring her was taking second place to the anxiety of not seeing it at all.

Three times Jessie lost her fuchsia-pink gloves, twice she tripped blithely off the pavement under the nose of a taxi and she *would* dawdle. "No need to get there *too* soon," she said happily at Liberty's window. "I've a feeling it will be very dull. Well, you know what I mean, dear, pepper and salt or lumpy porridge! Sweet of this man to ask us, but . . ."

Forty minutes later the "but" had vanished.

"Sweet of you to ask us— Mr.—er—" Jessie's hand, triumphantly gloved, rested daintly in that of her host, her eyes peeping charmingly from under her large-brimmed hat. The name she had been told several times, but names, Johanna was beginning to realize, went into the same category as "Look Left" notices—Jessie was above them. And—it had to be admitted—the tall Irishman seemed oblivious to everything but the effect of cornflower linen suit, fuchsia-pink hat and soupçon of amber fringe, the producer of which effect was now declaring barefacedly: "As I said to Jo coming along Regent Street, I'm *mad* about Irish tweed."

Nice man, she was thinking, lovely for Jo if he was a bit younger, anyway I suppose he's married. What a shame. Mum, will you never learn? Deb would say. But it's not wrong to want people to be happy, and little Jo's such a pet.

Beside her, as they were ushered into the exhibition hall, came a soft whisper: "Did someone say something about pepper and salt and porridge?"

Johanna could not only smile, she could sparkle. And, more than ever as Jessie looked at the close cap of nut-brown hair, the slender shoulders tanned to café-au-lait and the polka-dotted emerald shift the thought persisted: Yes, Deb, I do know I shouldn't, but if only she could meet some nice boy here to-day—why not?

"Porridge? If this is porridge?" Jo whispered again, "who'd go to work on an egg?"

Looking past her, Jessie saw why. There was the hall with its striking effects of white paint and sheer white curtains against nasturtium-coloured walls and matching carpet, the centrepiece of yellow and sunset roses, the dark couches and the square white coffee tables, and all round, hanging straight or carelessly draped, bright as a beacon, rich as a Mediterranean grotto, ripe as a cornfield, the lengths of Irish handwoven tweed.

Jessie's drooping jaw was the best appreciation she could have given, and the handsome Irishman marked it with gratification.

"You've seen nothing yet," he promised. "Come along." His hand went under her elbow.

Johanna lingered for a moment. She had an eye that went deeper than Jessie's, colour yes, the same dazzling impact—that turquoise blue, that blazing pink, that orange—but a bit more, the steps back into a country that in the past two weeks seemed to have closed its frontiers.

The turquoise was a variation of the honeycomb weave, the yarn had a knop of yellow and some green had been interwoven. Skilful dyeing too for just that shade of blue, fustic and indigo, she supposed, but so tender. How kind it would be to the wearer. The orange tweed was not just orange, it was a twill with fuchsia red in it. The pink was just as new, heavier and much softer, an irregular tabby and twill pattern in hot pink, lavender and scarlet. The dyes? Cochineal probably, suitably mordanted. She took it between her fingers, gazing at the crossings, terribly simple, almost what a child would do, terribly, terribly effective.

It was coming back like a voice . . . the weaves, the combinations, the colours, the dyes. Not the shock it had been to Jessie; she, Johanna, had known what modern Irish tweeds were like. Some of these designs were just like the ones Myles had been working on. Myles . . . she raised her eyes from the pink tweed and looked down the hall again.

The sign was waiting for her—or so it seemed. It was over a display not ten yards away.

## O'MALLEY TWEEDS LTD. CARRICKDOO.

Another Irishman, sales manager of one of the exhibitors, took them over. His name was Arthur Doyle and he had a silver tongue.

"To us, of course, tweed is a national heritage. We were making it when the rest of Europe were at each other's throats." His hearers, feeling almost responsible for the Goth hordes, nodded humbly.

"A long time ago," he allowed. "But it still sticks. Your Irishman nearly always has an eye for colour and a spark or two of poetry to go with it. As one of my competitors has it on their labels: 'The weaver has put something of his own character into this cloth, ruggedness for wear, softness for comfort and colours from our Donegal countryside. Joy and health to you who wear it.'

"The stand beside yours, Mr.—er—Doherty." Jessie sat up from the cosseting cushions to point, to Johanna's dismay, at the O'Malley sign. "I've been looking at it all the time. The colours really are glorious, aren't they, Jo?"

It was fair comment. Perhaps not to everybody's taste, certainly not those to whom tweed meant misty shades, but a triumph song in that the trends of the day had been so magically captured. The O'Malley stand under its sign—a sheep and a lamb grazing above a foam-flecked turquoise sea—sizzled with colour.

It had been drawing Johanna's eyes, but common sense warned her against it. Running away was one thing, putting your hand into the fire quite another. She'd applied for and been appointed to the post in Great Yarmouth and from now on all she wanted was the pale green peace of her homeland. That way it would have to end soon, the spinning dreadful whirlpool.

*Your fault, he needn't have been there, he was going to meet you.*

"Glorious," she said sparsely. To go down the floor and find herself in Myles's milieu and presumably amongst his family would "fix" the pain.

"Ah, that was a dreadful thing about young Myles O'Malley," Mr. Doyle said, shaking his head. "Only twenty-two and killed outright a couple of weeks ago in a car crash. There's a stretch on the Swords road—you wouldn't know it, of course—due north of Dublin on the main road to Belfast, and it seems to be a death-trap, though, knowing Myles pretty well, I'd say he wasn't going slowly."

Had her face blanched? Johanna could only hope desperately that it had not, especially as Jessie's eyes were now registering shocked recognition.

"The parents aren't over this time. I believe they're not well enough. Matt's got arthritis, of course, he'd hardly have come anyway, but I was just saying this morning, I don't remember a single other showing that Sheila wasn't at."

Jessie, warmhearted to a degree, was already making all the required expressions of sympathy. Thankful for it, Johanna sat still, staring frozenly at the O'Malley tweeds —stripes, checks, plaids, the diamond goose eye in black and white, and twills that verged from the classic herringbone to near-abstract compositions. Myles's designs, she'd know them anywhere. Yes indeed, though only now was it really hitting her, there was more to it than just the loss of a dear son.

"*He* designed most of those tweeds you see on the stand," their informant continued. "He'd have gone far, that lad. Makes it all the sadder."

And it was her fault.

"Like to take a look?" Mr. Doyle was inviting. "The brother should be somewhere around, Nice chap. It was hard on him too—having to come, I mean. He was telling me this morning that he felt like a fish out of water." He made to stand up.

*No!* Had she cried it aloud? It had felt like it, every nerve of her body screaming in revolt. No, I *don't* want to meet his brother. I couldn't bear it.

Happily, Johanna realized, she must have remained dumb, for it was Jessie—and another reason to be grateful to her—who was speaking, saying composedly: "Thanks so much, but I'd like to sit for a while longer if that's all right."

Mr. Doyle said gallantly that the longer they sat the better he'd be pleased and went off to see what drinks were going.

Jessie thought: "Another delightful man," and turned to Johanna to say so, but the face beside her was so strained that the words died on her lips. How unfortunate that the O'Malley tragedy should have come up like that just when the poor child had begun to perk up a bit. And how charming she looked in that rich green. If only some nice man—that nice *Mr. Doherty*, was it? she wished she were better at names—he was a good bit younger than John's connection, but . . .

"I suppose he's married," she said disgruntledly.

"*Married?*" Johanna was staring at her. "Who?"

"Him," said Jessie simply. "The man who's bringing our drinks."

"I don't care whether he's married or not," Johanna observed flatly, and instantly a new voice remarked: "*Cheeky!*"

"But since you mention it," it added. "Nobody's asked me yet."

The chirpiest smile Johanna had ever seen was bent upon them; its owner, slim as a whip, dark as a Moor and exquisitely tweed-clad, was holding in two hands and somewhat precariously two sherries and a large gin and tonic. "Sorry about that," he explained in tones which though lighter were as beguilingly Irish as Mr. Doyle's had been. "Art just got himself shanghaied." The glasses clinked softly on to the low white table. The bearer said fervently: "Thank God for that," and seated himself beside Johanna.

His hair, apart from its sideboards, was twin in cut to her own and there wasn't a hint of brown in it, it was the jettest of blacks. But the swarthy face beneath it was less ducal. A bold child's face, its charm was that it was instantly at home with you and you with it.

"Oh, sorry again. Forgot to introduce myself," the owner appended. "O'Malley, Shay O'Malley, at your service."

For a moment the world stood still. *Shay*—it must be a nickname, though Myles had never used it. Always he had referred to his brother as "Doug" and now the first thudding shock gave way to disbelief. Surely Douglas O'Malley who moved "only when pushed", who felt like "a fish out of water", could not look like this? She'd pictured him either spectacled and bookish or plumpish and lazy.

"And you?" Shay prompted, smiling.

"My friend is Mrs. Lee," she said steadily. "I'm— Johanna Dykes."

"Mrs. Lee." Shay shook Jessie's hand. "Nice to meet you. I just got a quick word from Art. You know X?" he mentioned the name of John Lee's friend and Jessie nodded beaming. A second later the same hand went warmly into Johanna's. "Greetings, Johanna. Where from?"

Johanna let go the breath she'd been holding. Obviously her name meant nothing to him, though for her his voice had now registered painfully. Two or three stunning

21

moments in a phone box on Norwich station and that voice had shattered her world. It was a voice quite similar to Myle's own, though with more of an accent. As indeed the brothers were heart-stirringly similar in looks—the same long legs, same black hair, same round jaw. Myles, however, had been handsome, Shay was engaging.

"Norfolk." She drew another breath. "Roughly midway between Norwich and Great Yarmouth."

A tiny pause and then the world stood still again. "Now what do I know about Great Yarmouth?" The dark head went to one side and the round eyes—dark brown where Myles's had been blue—considered. "Got it! David Copperfield and bloaters. Right?"

Relief was such that she bubbled into laughter.

Shay took her round the stands. Even to an untutored eye it would have been engrossing, to Johanna it brought more and more the sense of renewal she'd had on entry.

Here within the last decade a whole new world had exploded, and how skilfully the designers were shaping it. One stand showed heavy tweeds that had almost a "darned" finish. Another had a coarse interlacing effect, inspired, Shay told her, by the creels used for the peat. It had been made up with a twist of sunset pink and orange crossing one of parma and olive green. She took a hectic handful in her grasp and it was soft as a blanket.

"That's your good bog water," Shay said complacently, and proceeded to explain how advantageous this was in the washing and shrinking processes. He had shown a new gravity since they'd started the tour of inspection.

Shay talked well and seriously about the need for good designers. They were, he said, a prerequisite for export expansion, and he instanced a pilot scheme for the employment of consultant stylists which the Irish Export Board had initiated. Several firms had already participated.

"We'll need to do something about it soon," he ended quietly. "We've just lost our best designer."

Said so simply, it took her by surprise. Once again she felt her cheeks burn. "Yes, I—I know. Mr. Doyle told us. I'm—very sorry."

The dark eyes held a look that to her over-sensitive nerves seemed questioning. "Thanks," Shay said. "It was a bad business. In fact I don't quite know how we'll make out without him.

It was something Myles would never have voiced. He'd been confident about everything, his designs, his parents—and her. He had chosen and moved in and that was the end of it. He had never doubted his powers. And at the wheel of a car he had never doubted his judgment. But there had been just one time when it hadn't been good enough, and so he'd never known that another occasion was coming up which would have disproved his faith—his faith in the girl he'd chosen.

Normally at this point the dreaded whirlpool would take over her thoughts. Now it didn't. She stood there looking at Shay's young mobile face and feeling suddenly protective.

Almost as though he'd read her, Shay suggested that they should go outside for a minute and get some fresh air. After the exhibition hall it was pleasantly cool in the little concrete patch at the rear which served as a car park. Shay pulled on his cigarette as though the day's efforts and the barrage of sales talk had taken their toll.

"Not in the way that's wanted," he said in reply to Johanna's question as to whether he did any designing himself. "I can draft patterns, but someone must give me the picture." He rested his elbows on the roof of a white Mercedes with an IRL plate up and stared moodily across it.

Johanna thought first, what a field it would be, and then with a dart of excitement, *Could I do it? Could I help out?*

It seemed like an answer. She looked at the muscular shoulders in the fine tweed suiting, the cream silk shirt and the long golden-brown floral tie. "You've to do with Sales, though, haven't you?" she asked.

"At the moment. But only because this thing happened along and no one else was available. I'm odd job man really. Originally a weaver, but I've been round all the departments."

Another surprise. The very last impression Myles had given of his brother was that he'd worked his way from the ranks.

"And how has to-day gone? Or shouldn't I ask?" she

23

ventured, and leaned in her turn against the sporty Irish car.

"Of course." He gave her again that intimate smile. "It's gone quite well, thanks, but there's been one big disappointment. At least it looks that way now." Johanna waited. Unlikely that he would be specific. After all, he'd never laid eyes on her until an hour ago. And yet she felt so close to him and so involved. "I suppose you could call it the one that got away," Shay was saying ruefully. "Yesterday I thought he was in the boat. A real ninety-pounder." And he went on to elucidate. The "fish" had been a buyer from a big department store controlling a chain throughout the country. They sold their own garments under a brand name and had them made up under contracts. Now they were looking for tweed to be used in a range of ladies' coats, frocks and blouses. The designs which would be exclusive to them had to be of a really exclusive character. "Mind you, as things are, I'm not sure if we could have done it," Shay confessed. "though I wouldn't at all have minded having a stab. Anyway I haven't clapped eyes on him to-day and I don't think he's coming back now."

A man came in and stood looking at them, a stocky man with wind-blown brownish hair. The other men present had almost seemed to vie with each other in the matter of smart suitings, pastel shirts and subtly shaded neckties. His clothes were plain, a grey crew-necked sweater, old slacks and a grey tweed sports jacket.

"You're wanted, Shay," he said, and his voice was quiet.

"Oh, lor', who?" Shay straightened himself wearily.

"Felgate-Winter." The tone was laconic, but Shay's response to it anything but that. *"Felgate-Winter?"* He dropped his cigarette and ground it into the concrete apron. You did not need to be clairvoyant to divine that yesterday's "fish" had returned.

His excitement showing in his face, Shay grasped Johanna's hand. "Keep your fingers crossed, Jo, this is it. And thanks for letting me talk. You've been a sport." He hesitated for a second, his warm olive-skinned face alight, his long legs looking as though they had been poured into the exaggeratedly narrow trousers. The grey

24

man, still in the background, had sturdy legs and she had seldom seen anyone look so impassive. Had he really said "Shay?" He looked like a storeman or a plain clothes constable.

"Good luck," she said tremulously as Shay got to the door and he waved and ducked inside.

Johanna and the grey stranger were left alone. It seemed a moment when somebody should say something, but he showed no sign of doing so. On second glance he had an air about him; head well set, jaw broad, chest powerful. A tree-trunk man, she thought fancifully. She said on impulse: "The tweeds are fabulous, aren't they? And the colours. Particularly on the O'Malley stand."

The voice was as quiet as before. It was also as sparing of itself. "Thank you," it said.

*Thank you.* Then he must be an employee—perhaps privileged to use Shay's christian name because they'd worked together on the factory floor.

"Oh yes," she stressed warmly. "I've got stacks to remember. I . . ." and stopped short.

The eyes had looked into hers politely but with a quite obvious disinterest. She had time to notice that they were a clear dark grey and as serious as the rest of him.

"Goodnight," he said firmly, and brushed past her.

It wasn't that she cared, it wasn't that it mattered . . . and you'd think she was much too sick and sore about Myles even to notice . . . but even before she'd met Myles, well, you couldn't help knowing when people liked you, and as for getting the brush-off, well, never in her life, until now.

And why it should hurt—she'd thought after Myles that nothing like that would ever hurt her again—she didn't know, but as she stood there looking after the stocky figure walking so unconcernedly away from her, brown head erect, back straight, weight slightly on the heels, she knew that she was smarting from head to toe.

## CHAPTER THREE

IT WAS a case of not stopping to think in case she'd get cold feet, and at that they were fast overtaking her. It could be safely said that when the stewardess's voice came over the speaker on the plane the butterflies in one passenger's tummy had nothing to do with the mechanics of take-off.

The stewardess repeated in English what she had already said in Irish: It began: "Aer Lingus Irish welcome you aboard their Viscount St. Colman," and ended: "We hope you will enjoy the flight." The luggage truck, now empty, chugged back to base and the propellors spun.

Too late now, Johanna thought, am I crazy? A holiday job, she'd told her parents, had come up in Dublin. "Oh, darling, no!" For once her mother had not been detached. "You've had your exams and the shock over Myles. We don't want you to think of working this summer." But crazy or not, melodramatic or not, here she was.

A stewardess in short-sleeved primrose shirt and the green skirt of her uniform emerged from the galley with a basket of glucose sweets and passed it smilingly to each passenger. The plane taxied down the runway, halted for clearance and, a few minutes later, was airborne. A perfect take-off so smooth that few passengers seemed to have even noticed it. No reason at all, the stewardess thought, for that girl in the marigold linen suit to sit so far forward gripping the arms of her seat. But then the stewardess did not know that the first stage of Johanna's pilgrimage had begun.

It went on peacefully, coming in to land over tongues of emerald green limned round with deep brown sand and a patchwork of small fields dotted with cattle and heavily fleeced buff sheep, going through the usual formalities at the airport and boarding the coach for Dublin. At the city terminal she changed to a taxi which brought her at the speed of crawl through lunch hour traffic to her final destination, a quiet non-licensed hotel near a Victorian-Gothic church whose silver-grey steeple seemed to shimmer against the deep cobalt sky.

In the hotel room, she found a telephone directory and dialled. Answer was prompt. "Good afternoon. O'Malley Tweeds Ltd. Can I help you?"

"May I speak to Mr. Shay O'Malley, please?" Johanna asked.

"I'm sorry, Mr. O'Malley is in Donegal."

Johanna moistened her lips. "Will he be in tomorrow?"

"No. We're not expecting him back till the end of the week. Will anyone else do?"

"I . . ." Johanna hesitated and swallowed. "Yes. Could I make an appointment to see Mrs. O'Malley?"

The premises of O'Malley Tweeds Ltd. in Kellard Street were only a stone's throw from the Victorian-Gothic church with its flying buttresses and its little grey cloister. The street ran down from the church railings to the white-marked traffic lanes in broad College Green.

O'Malley House, a polygon, stood out boldly from the other buildings in the street. Its purplish brown bricks were faced with white stone, its wavy entrance canopy on slim grey pillars gave it the look of a pavilion. All over, it was a shock, but an exhilarating one.

In its window three drapes of tweed came to rest on a carpet of dull olive green. One drape was heather pink, the second purple, the third deep violet. A pale mauve blouse with a neck band lay on the purple length. In the centre of the carpet sat a petal cloche shaded in the violet and purple with touches of hyacinth and pink. Someone had obviously worked hard to get away from the trade image.

Behind the plate glass door lay a new world, new people, new ground; not too fanciful to describe it as enemy territory. Indeed the abstract design embellishing the door suggested spearheads. Wisdom even at this eleventh hour began to make noises—she was carrying a time bomb; even the one friendly face, Shay's would be friendly no longer if he knew the truth. But strangely, for all that, it was also a beckoning country, in a way a Promised Land.

To have found the usual counter and enquiry hatch would have been disappointing. She didn't. It was a small bright honeycomb with cream walls, cream tweed on the settee, black doors and a red carpet. The desk was low level and cream-topped.

"Oh yes, Miss Dykes," the girl in charge of it murmured, and lifted a cream telephone. "I'll just ring Miss Baldwin."

"My appointment," Johanna said apprehensively, "is with Mrs. O'Malley."

27

"Well, yes." A touch of hesitation. "But Miss Baldwin usually . . . I mean . . . she's her secretary."

Johanna caught her breath. They'd probably concluded that she was selling carbon paper or canvassing for entries in a directory. "I'm sorry, but I must see Mrs. O'Malley."

The blue eyes behind the desk looked somewhat harassedly into hers.

"If you like I'll ask Miss Baldwin."

Johanna opened her mouth indignantly and closed it again. Remembering that Sheila O'Malley had not been well enough to go to the exhibition, this small pony-tailed dragon became less infuriating, the more so as she suddenly confessed: "Sorry, I have to do this. Miss Baldwin's orders." She didn't quite pull a face, she straightened it just in time. A minute later the smile was back, this time conspiratorial. "You're in luck. Miss Baldwin's out and Mrs. O'Malley says will you go in." The way she indicated briefly. "Down the passage, second door on the right. Sorry I can't leave the desk."

True Johanna hadn't known the way, truer that she'd loitered because her knees had shown a tendency to buckle. The sense of Myles's presence had never been so strong. He must have often passed the little dragon, gone down this low-ceilinged pale corridor with the opaque wall lights like portholes and stood, as she was standing now, at the closed door of his mother's office.

She raised her hand and tapped on the door. "Come in," a voice bade.

The handle turned easily, the door slid over a stained glass patterned carpet. Johanna saw a desk, empty, and an aluminum framed window, open. The room's only occupant, tall, slim and redhaired, in a sleeveless dress, was standing by the window sipping a glass of water.

"Take a seat, Miss Dykes, I'll be with you in a moment."

A little dazedly Johanna did so, letting her eyes dwell on the room to keep them from hanging too obviously on the youthful form of Myles's mother. Easy to see where Shay and Myles had got their whip-slim grace. Sheila O'Malley must have been at least in the late forties, but she could have passed for thirty-seven. Her hair curved like a flame into her slim neck, her legs were long and slender. The high-necked dress of coarse weave linen was seaweed-brown.

She had returned by now to the long spreading desk, set down the empty glass and was putting a phial of capsules back into a drawer. "Now, Miss Dykes, if this won't take too long—I can give you . . ." A glance at her wristwatch. "About five minutes. Right?"

"I do appreciate your seeing me, Mrs. O'Malley. It's very good of you."

"I understood from my secretary that it was very important." A quizzical light gleamed momentarily in the brown eyes.

"Yes," Johanna swallowed, "it is. I—I'm a student."

Another keen amused glance. "You don't look like one!"

Johanna smiled hesitantly. Was she being jeered at or challenged? Or paid a compliment? With Sheila O'Malley it would never be easy to tell. She began awkwardly to explain that she had thought of making a holiday study of handwoven tweed. "You see—I love it."

The admission drew another smile. "Then you've come to the right place. Did you want to visit our factory?"

A start and Johanna grasped it. "Oh, could I? Now?"

The smile broadened as the neat head shook. "It's not here, you know. It's in Donegal. This is our H.Q., and nerve centre." It seemed an apt term, for as she spoke the telephone shrilled. "Excuse me." She raised the receiver. The conversation took about three minutes. It had something to do with "Cloth 14." "It's not going to do, Harry," Sheila said firmly. "I don't like it." Listening, Johanna had a cold feeling. How could you offer help to someone so poised and able? "Well, if you like, though I can't see what good it's going to do," Sheila O'Malley was concluding discouragingly. "And give me five minutes. I've got someone with me at the moment." As she replaced the phone it rang again. She spoke, presumably, to the exchange operator, "No, she's not back yet. Put them on."

Once more Johanna listened, this time to what seemed like a conversation with a travel agency. Rome was mentioned and Sheila O'Malley drew the leather desk calendar closer and frowned at it. "Yes, all right. Now about

29

Frankfurt?" The brows, darkened to a chestnut brown, straightened again. "Yes, fine—get me on that.

"I'm sorry, Miss Dykes. As you see I don't really have a lot of spare time," she said smoothly, replacing the receiver. "Now can we get you sorted? Donegal. Have you a car?"

No chance of getting a word in. Johanna, having shaken her head, found herself listening to details of the Express Bus Service. "You can see the factory any day except Saturday. We work a five-day week. Ask for Mr. Grogan and tell him you've been to see me. I should perhaps warn you that in Carrickdoo we make the beam, that's the warp . . ." Johanna nodded, "and wind the weft threads on to the cops. Then it goes out to the weaver."

"You mean, it really is still done in the cottages?"

"Well, of course." Again the note of amusement. "What did you think? We're not a pack of confidence tricksters, you know." The voice rose a tone and Johanna felt herself colour. Sheila O'Malley for all her attractiveness had a sharpness about her that could be disconcerting. However, she was now continuing more kindly, "It's entirely piece work and the men fit it in with their other jobs. They're mostly hill farmers, you see, and they can do this quite easily. Life doesn't change much up there." There was a new note in her voice. You could almost call it wistfulness. But next instant she was as brisk as ever. "Well, that's settled, then. I hope you'll find it useful."

Dismissal was now very definitely in the air. Now or never, Johanna thought, opened her mouth and closed it again. If she could only know which was right, the picture Shay had painted or the all-sufficient impression his mother gave. Was any reparation needed? Had she been a fool to come?

"Oh, I daresay you'd like some patterns," Sheila O'Malley was saying. "And we have brief notes we're sometimes asked for by students. I'll just see if my secretary has come back." She lifted the cream telephone again and dialled a number with the end of her pencil.

In a moment good-byes would be said and Johanna would be shown out with nothing achieved. Panic washing over her, she plunged.

"Mrs. O'Malley, before I go I was wondering . . ."

"Yes?" Johanna caught a hint of raggedness. Had it come, she queried, from a build-up of tension? Trying to fit sixteen hours' work into eight and a half and not helped by time-wasters like herself? Sheila O'Malley was not so girlish if you peered below the surface. A pent-up look sometimes showed, deepening the lines round her mouth, and Johanna had noticed that the slim hands had to be busy. They had now picked up a strip of gossamer patterns and were pulling it through their fingers. "It was just . . ." Johanna looked at the hands rather than the face. "I thought—could I work for you for a week or two?"

The hands answered her. Sheila O'Malley pulled the white and salmon pink squares taut and seemed also to tauten herself. "I'm afraid not," she said flatly. "We have absolutely no employment to offer students."

"I wouldn't want payment," Johanna blurted. "Just to help."

"Help?" Again the rise in tone and now also a rise in brow. "What could you do?"

It was all going wrong anyway, so she couldn't make it much worse. "I thought I could design."

"*Design*?" The hardest to bear was the light laugh. "Just like that?" Silence, almost a lingering note of sadness. The brown eyes travelled uncannily to the photograph.

"Oh, Mrs. O'Malley, I know you think it's cheek, but I do have a feeling for tweed. I love it." The words tumbled. "A natural feeling for cloth," one of her instructors had put it, though, granted, he had been referring to the designs she had put forward for printing. "Even if I didn't love you I'd still take you home. You'll go over big with the folks," Myles had said once, more valuably.

"My dear child," the patient voice cut into her reflections, "I don't doubt you, but I'm afraid love isn't enough. Our styling is the work of an international team, all of them with years of experience. Perhaps some day you might be one of them, who knows? But not today, I'm afraid. After all, you're still learning to walk." There was again that sudden note of kindness and Johanna felt her eyes held by the other brown ones. "I'm not blaming you, no, I'm *not*. On the contrary I feel flattered that you

31

chose to come here. Why did you? A pin in a list of names?" She was poised again and amused.

"No, Mrs. O'Malley," said Johanna. "I came because of your son."

The smile was wiped away, the face became bleak as an ice floe. The eyes dilated. "You knew my son?"

*Past* tense, and it jerked Johanna to the edge of her own pit. Myles, not Shay! Sheila O'Malley, looking at her like that, was thinking of Myles, asking if she had known him . . . could they possibly know or guess why Myles had been going to Scotland? Her head began to reel.

It was the first occasion to require a downright lie. "Not Myles. I never knew him." To give it was suddenly impossible. But in that second the door opened and two people made simultaneous entry, a middle-aged man carrying a piece of tweed and exclaiming: "Sorry, Sheila, I thought you were finished. Shall I go?" and a tall girl with papers in her hand. She gave her employer one look and asked urgently: "Mrs. O'Malley, are you all right?" Effectually drowning reply to either question came the telephone ringing again.

The girl, dark-haired, blue-eyed, willowy and wearing a dress in a curious weave of thin stripes, clicked her tongue as she answered it. "Good morning. Mrs. O'Malley's office. No, this is Geraldine Baldwin, her secretary. May I call you back?"

Shaken as she was, Johanna remembered the little receptionist and the face she'd all but pulled when she'd said: "Miss Baldwin." Prejudice, she accused herself sharply. Despite this, the thought remained. And meantime, as suddenly as she had relinquished it, Sheila O'Malley re-took command.

"No, Harry, stay. Miss Dykes, were you speaking of my son Myles?"

Something she could deny and with truth. Relieved, she did so. "Oh no, your other son. I met him just a week ago at the London exhibition." It was puzzling that the cloud now seemed to have settled on Geraldine Baldwin. As she continued Johanna felt the blue eyes appraise her. "He told me about his brother's accident. I understood a lot of the designs were his," Johanna ploughed on. "And

32

Mr. O'Malley seemed anxious about the future. I couldn't help thinking about it, wondering if I could help, and—in the end I came."

Sheila O'Malley repeated her previous reaction, a headshake and a little incredulous laugh: "Just like that?"

"It was foolish. I know that now," Johanna said hastily. "I didn't understand you had so many other designers." She never would understand, she thought helplessly, but one thing was clear. Whatever Shay had meant there was after all no gap she could fill. "Please forgive me for having taken up so much of your time, and thank you for seeing me." She stood up.

"Miss Dykes, I'm puzzled. It doesn't sound like my son." Sheila O'Malley's brown eyes were still fixed on her and across the room Geraldine Baldwin's watched her too, apprehensively if that were possible. Johanna, looking away from them, tried to explain. "We went outside to talk. He seemed tired and he told me about some big order he was hoping for. That was my reason for coming. I thought . . ."

As she paused the man "Harry" rushed in: "Exactly, Sheila. If we're doing 'Young O'Malley' we need ideas as new and as young as tomorrow. This young lady's the right age to have them. It's worth a try."

"I don't think so." The cool voice of Myles' mother did not waver. She looked back at Johanna. "There's nothing definitely fixed about 'Young O'Malley' and I'm sorry if my son raised your hopes . . ."

Johanna, wondering wildly what 'Young O'Malley' was, made an attempt to speak, but was again cut short by Harry. "Ah, that's wrong, Sheila. You should give the boy a chance occasionally. After all, *he* landed the fish." He paused and Geraldine Baldwin cut in swiftly and with a frown. "Please, Mr. Blake, not now." Her glance towards her employer was meaningful.

"I must be going," Johanna said awkwardly.

"I am sorry about this, Miss Dykes, but I'm afraid it doesn't alter the position. We don't need a young designer." Sheila O'Malley's eyes were concerned, Harry Blake's mutinous and Geraldine Baldwin's patently and incomprehensibly relieved. "However, this I will do. If you're likely to be in Dublin till the end of the week I'll arrange transport for you to see the factory. If you'll leave your address with Miss Baldwin she'll get in touch with you." A cool handshake accompanied the smile. Johanna returned both and allowed herself to be ushered into the corridor.

In Reception Geraldine Baldwin took down the name of the hotel, but not before she had had a word with "the little dragon." "Betty, you're still not putting Mrs. O'Malley's calls through to me."

"I hope I didn't upset her," Johanna ventured anxiously. "I knew she hadn't been well, but I thought since she was back at work . . ."

This was instantly derided. "That doesn't mean anything. Of course she's not fit. How could she be after the trouble she's had!" The ballpoint pen went almost through the paper with the zeal of its holder's views. "You just have to think for Mrs. O'Malley these days because the last person she thinks of is herself. And they're hopeless at the desk, they send up *anybody*."

To this there seemed no answer, partly because the receptionist was within hearing, partly because Johanna divined the hit at herself.

"Right, Miss Dykes." The last savage stroke was drawn and Geraldine Baldwin slipped the note into her jotter. "*If* there's a car going up we'll let you know." It was rather different from Sheila O'Malley's promise, but the tone would have quelled a stouter heart than Johanna's. She said a respectful: "Thank you," and made for the door.

"Was it all right?" a voice enquired. "Or did Lady Muck stick her oar in?"

"No, indeed. Mrs. O'Malley was very kind," Johanna said, smiling. Somehow you couldn't help it.

"Oh, *she* would be, *she's* all right," the other agreed, and added confidingly, "She's not really. She ought to be home in bed. You know, shock and everything."

Johanna's distant nod was no deterrent. The last lugubrious comment had to come. "God love her, she idol*ised* him—brat though he was."

There are some resolutions beyond anyone's power to keep. Johanna's "Brat?" quickly stifled, just got out.

Response was ready.

"The son. Myles. The one that just got himself killed.

34

Well, you know what I mean, don't you . . ." She had the typical Irish eyes, sparkling and wicked. "Taking letters, he never let you sit on the far side of the desk! Honestly, once or twice, I thought I'd *die*!"

## CHAPTER FOUR

THE interview with Sheila O'Malley had taken place on Tuesday and by Saturday morning no further word had come. Nor would it now, Johanna acknowledged sadly, since "the end of the week" had been the set time limit. And yet for all the times she told herself this, it was countered compulsively by another thought: "You never know. She might still. If only I could afford to wait!" And then inspiration! Why couldn't she? Surely somewhere in Dublin there was a job that would keep her for a week or two. Breakfast over, she ran out and bought a morning paper.

And there before her eyes, three insertions from the top of the *Situations Vacant* page, and hardly possible to be plainer or more unvarnished—Johanna grabbed the paper and held it closer.

"Required urgently. Temporary cook-housekeeper, three adults, other help kept. References essential. O'Malley, Knockbeg, Blackglen, Kilmashogue."

The terseness gave it impact, made the phrases jump. *Required urgently. Cook-housekeeper. O'Malley, Knockbeg, Kilmashogue.* Myles's address, the house she'd telephoned from Norwich. And *required urgently.* Illness? The reason why she hadn't heard from Sheila O'Malley?

A few hours later Johanna looked sternly at her reflection in the bus window and told it not to be a baby. Somewhat dimly in the dusty glass her face looked back at her, pink ear-lobes under a soft flop of hair, slim throat rising from a cream polo shirt. An irksomely transparent face.

Reassurance—how desperately she needed it, and how strangely devoid of it the telephone conversation with Shay O'Malley had been. She'd pinned her hopes on him,

35

but if she had not asked specifically for "Mr. O'Malley Junior", and if the voice had not immediately said: "Yes, speaking," she would have thought she'd got the wrong person. No trace at all of the bantering warmth that had been so disarming at the exhibition. To-day's voice had been subdued and businesslike.

Indeed, yes, the post was still open and he would be glad to discuss it with her, "Miss—er—Dykes." It had not been Miss Dykes at the exhibition, it had been "Johanna" or "Jo", yet when she'd begun this morning by: "Mr. O'Malley, this is Johanna Dykes," the only reaction had been a polite: "Oh yes?"

"You probably don't remember me," she'd fumbled embarrassedly, "But we have met—at the exhibition in London." There had been a moment of disconcerting silence and then again, even more disconcertingly, had come: "Oh yes." Deflating, even extraordinary, but plain he had absolutely no recollection of her. The tone though was conciliatory as though he disliked giving offence. "I met such a lot of people. I'm sorry."

Still in that quiet serious tone he had given her directions. "Go through Rathnasee village and turn left, then right at the Yellow House and left again at the Tuning Fork. Continue for about three-quarters of a mile to Grange crossroads and turn left." If he had said: "Stay in the bus till the terminus," it would have been simpler.

"Now, love," the conductor was leaning over her seat, "when we stop you want to go up to the left. 'Bouta half a mile there's a crossroads. Black Glen goes on straight."

A cold shiver ran down her spine as the bus rounded its last corner and then—the first thing she saw was the sunshine, the second the hills. A well-kept secret, how they burst upon her, dwarfing the little shops and cottages that clustered round the terminus.

Johanna's slim form, looking in its brief marigold suit not strikingly like the Israelite scout, but, nevertheless, one of his descendants, went up the steep road on winged feet.

For the half mile or so the bus conductor had mentioned it was quite a climb.

Black Glen—was there ever such a misnomer?—went carelessly south east with the sunshine behind it, and

Johanna, going with it, came suddenly on three or four parked cars and a gate bearing the name Knockbeg.

Beyond the gate, a branching drive, massed pink and orange roses and the house, a new ranch type bungalow with a dormer floor; cream-washed, red brick facings, lots of glass. Her eye, travelling swiftly, noted the exterior staircase which apparently gave access to the dormer floor, the little balcony reached through a glass door also in the dormer storey, the two garages, and the right arm of the driveway leading to a small detached building too big and solid for a summer house.

She watched, guessing, as the door opened and a woman emerged carrying a basket. As she passed Johanna a resentful "Meow" sounded, and she smiled and hurried to one of the parked cars. Simultaneously another car decanted two small boys and a dog. They too went through the gate of Knockbeg. And then Johanna noticed the small bronze plate on the gatepost.

### "D. L. O'Malley, M.R.C.V.S."

D. L. O'Malley. Douglas O'Malley, the brother who took no part in the tweed business. Hardly to be wondered at, Johanna conceded, if he were a vet, but rather different from the impression Myles had given.

"Excuse me, please." The shrill pipe belonged to one of the two small boys. "Are you looking for Mr. O'Malley? It's this way."

He pushed the door of the detached building. Inside, in a green tiled waiting-room, a tall youngster in her early teens was nursing a black toy poodle and a small boy with an untidy cap of dark hair was sprawled over a table flicking through a magazine. An inner door led presumably to the surgery.

"Aren't you coming in?" the elder boy of Johanna's escort asked.

She wasn't and she regretted it. It obviously was not the place to find Shay, but its "children's day" atmosphere was attractive.

"Right, Linda! Wheel her in!" a voice called informally through the surgery door. "How's she doing?"

"Great, Mr. O'Malley, she's lost four ounces," the tall

girl reported as she stowed the poodle under her arm and rose. The fidgety little boy also rose and followed to peep hopefully round the door.

"Not you again, Mark!" Johanna heard as she stepped back into the drive. "Did someone put the clock on in your house last night?"

Douglas O'Malley sounded quite nice enough to be Myles's and Shay's brother. He would look like them too, tall, slim and dark. She wondered idly whether he were blue-eyed like Myles or brown-eyed like Shay. It was clear now that, unspecific as Myles had been, he had had two brothers, not one, and—approaching it, her woman's eyes approved it again—a charming home, sparkling sunlit glass, wrought iron balcony, brick enclosed rose beds. The hall door, akin to the incised glass in the door of O'Malley House, was very pretty, but disappointingly her onslaughts on it produced only two musical notes and then complete silence.

She stood irresolute for a few minutes and retraced her steps to the surgery. It was after all conceivable that Shay had left word for her there.

"Now, then, who's next?" Douglas O'Malley called as his last "customer" left the surgery, and Johanna saw advancing a stocky white-coated figure.

She felt her jaw drop. The gay dark face she'd envisaged—there wasn't a trace of it. Instead, and for a moment she thought she was seeing things, the face was fair-skinned, blunt, heavy-jowled, with serious grey eyes. The "grey man" at the exhibition, the one who, perhaps unconsciously, had made her feel so small—*he* was Douglas O'Malley! It was the one explanation that had never crossed her mind.

"Well, Miss—er . . . what can I do for you? Cat, dog, rabbit, hamster, budgerigar, pony—take your pick!" The bantering tone was precisely the one he had used to the children and their pets.

She tried to match it. "Housekeeper!"

"Housekeeper?" he parried, and checked. "*House-keeper! You?*"

Johanna tried not to look at the widening eyes and the dropping jaw.

"Yes. We—er—have an appointment."

38

"You're not . . ." Again words seemed to fail him. "Johanna Dykes."

"But that's absolutely absurd," he said flatly. "I'm looking for someone with experience. I made that clear."

"But as you haven't got anybody and it's urgent," Johanna tried delicately, "I thought I might fill the gap."

"I see," he said, and this time more gently, "Sorry, but it's not on. This is a tough job, Miss Dykes, I make no bones about it. It needs a tough person."

"Would it help," she swallowed; this wasn't a lie, not the way she was going to put it, "if I were a Domestic Economy student?"

"It would only help," he declared with a faint smile, "if you were a forty-year-old one."

Not the kind of man, Johanna realized, with whom you argued. You might as well try to move one of the boulders on top of the mountain. It was another rebuff to her dream, and suddenly she saw how impossible the dream had been. She'd come on a wild goose chase, she'd been intrusive, idiotic.

But there was one thing you could not do and that was push in where you were not wanted.

She said resignedly: "That's that, then. I'm sorry for taking up your time."

In front of her, blocking the way to the door, Douglas O'Malley was sheer bulk, the white linen coat baying over the wide chest, the face from smoothed brown hair to jaw a solid oblong. A phrase strayed to mind, "the compleat angler"—here was surely the complete man. The slings and arrows of outrageous fortune would find him quite impervious. It was also benign bulk. She felt that very strongly.

"Look, sit down," the quiet voice bade her. "Let me explain."

"Cigarette?" he pushed the case across the table, remarking when she shook her head, "Good. I hate to see a child of your age taking it up." It did not stop him, she noticed, from taking one himself and drawing his lips into a whistling shape as he pulled on it.

"I'm not exactly a child," she said defensively. "I'm twenty."

"Twenty," he repeated gravely. "And you're a student. Where from?"

"Lond—Norwich." She saved herself quickly.

"Norwich?" The grey eyes had narrowed. "That's interesting."

She jerked like a puppet. "Why?" and she felt the colour flood her cheeks.

"My brother had friends living some miles out of Norwich. He told me about the country and how different it was from his. I suppose you found that coming here?"

She managed to squeak: "Yes," cleared her throat and said it again with more success. "Do you know their name?" she even managed to falter.

"Who? Oh, the friends'? No." Douglas O'Malley shook his head. Surprisingly, it was lightly frosted with grey at each temple. "Myles had so many we gave up keeping track long ago." And he sighed. The sigh, though unstressed, nevertheless pierced her. It was the kind of moment that brought home, if not in the way he had intended, at least the truth of his assertion that the job needed a tough person. She was not tough. It took just about all she had to say: "Was that the brother who met with the accident? I heard about it at the exhibition."

"Oh yes," now he was remembering her. "I saw you there, didn't I? You liked our tweeds."

"Very much."

The eyes had narrowed again and the head was tilted questioningly.

"That's a coincidence, isn't it? Our meeting in London and now here."

The complete man, she thought uneasily, was another way of saying that Douglas O'Malley was no fool. What was going on behind that big quiet face? She drew another breath.

"Not altogether. The exhibition decided me to come to Dublin to do a research project on tweed and then I read your advertisement. I read it by chance, but I came because it said required urgently and I wanted to help."

"But why?"

"At the exhibition everyone was talking about your brother," Johanna said simply. "And your mother. I felt sorry."

Across the table the grey eyes levelled with her own dark ones. "It was a nice thought," their owner said softly. "Thank you. I wish the right person would have it," he added somewhat tactlessly. "My mother keeps asking—she worries over my father being on his own. And Shay and I can't always be here, so it's quite a problem. My mother, of course, is in a nursing home at the moment. We've all seen it coming, my brother's death was a terrible blow to her, and she never gave way to it, at least not that any of us ever saw. And of course," he continued slowly, "sooner or later that kind of grief becomes a canker. If you don't let it out it eats in."

"Oh yes!" No one knew that better than herself. Even the bare mechanics of planning the journey to Dublin and what she'd done so far had helped. An outlet, selfish rather than selfless, but still an outlet, had been achieved. And now to her surprise the words went on: "But sometimes sitting down and crying about it doesn't do any good either. That happened to—a friend of mine. She couldn't talk about it, she just had to do things."

Another odd pause, shortlived but marked. Douglas O'Malley's eyes were once more fixed on her face, quietly but so searchingly that she felt exactly like one of his patients.

"Yes, well, you're right, of course," he agreed. "Except that in my mother's case she'd been trying to do fifty million things and all at once. So naturally nature caught up. Now tell me," his tone had subtly changed, "what do you know about running a house?"

Astonishment, breathtaking and incredulous, took hold of her. He was reconsidering. He was going to give her a chance. Something had changed him. What? She'd never know, and it didn't matter. Joyously, she launched into her case. A good one. Quite honestly, a good one. It had always been accepted at Dykes Lynn that her mother should have as much time as possible for her painting. Johanna had been cooking meals since she was ten. And not just snacks, she pointed out hastily, there was always good food on the farm and very frequently extra mouths to eat it.

He listened to it all, stroking his cheek in a thoughtful way.

"I see," he said when she'd finished. "Now there is one other point, Miss Dykes. As I mentioned, my father has arthritis and doesn't get into work these days. It's a virulent form, I'm sorry to say, and he suffers a great deal. It makes him short-tempered and impatient. Ideally whoever I engage should also have experience of invalids."

"I have," Johanna stated hopefully. "My grandfather lived with us for a year before he died, and he had the widest vocabulary in the county. Especially when it was going to rain!"

Something about Douglas O'Malley's smile made her feel much less than twenty and again very like a kitten or a puppy. Then the smile went and he sat looking at her, his right hand pulling absently at the lobe of his ear. "I don't know," he said at last. "I'm sorry. I just don't know."

Quietly spoken as always, did the man never raise his voice, she wondered, and then wham! Fists were beating the door panel in a violent tattoo. The handle turned, the door opened a few inches, a voice enquired: "Any of my enemies around, or is it safe to come in?" and a round swarthy face capped in black hair poked cautiously into the room.

Next instant the mouth had opened into an "O" of astonishment and Shay's slim form in sweater, slacks and canvas sneakers, a kitbag over one shoulder, was in the room. "Jo! I don't believe it. Are you real?" The kitbag dropped, arms caught her warmly in a boyish hug. "You *are*. Good man, Anthony!" he said exuberantly.

"Anthony?" Johanna echoed, staring at the teasing twinkling face.

"Pal of mine. Private eye. Best in the business," Shay declared merrily. "I retained him the day after the exhibition."

"You don't mean—looking for me?" Johanna stuttered.

"Who else? Desperate situations require desperate remedies."

"But . . ."

The almost black eyes only sparkled the more delightedly.

"St. Anthony," a quiet voice volunteered, "is this country's lost property officer."

"I really did try to find you," Shay was saying. "Art Doyle was to get your friend's address, but the chappie that knew it went on holiday the very next day, so it had to be Anthony, bless him. He did his stuff."

"Except that, funnily enough," Douglas O'Malley broke in again, "he sent her to the wrong man. Miss Dykes is here to see me." He looked at them both as a St. Bernard might regard a chihuahua, benevolent and heavily playful. Then he began to explain about the housekeeping job. As might have been expected, Shay was enthusiastic.

"It's not decided yet," Douglas reminded him. "I'm not sure that it would be fair to Miss Dykes."

"Jo," Shay corrected promptly. "She hates being called Miss Dykes."

It sounded so like Myles that Johanna was momentarily silent. "May I?" The grey eyes were fixed courteously on her. She said confusedly: "Oh—oh yes, please do." It was disconcerting, however, that Shay did not press the matter of the job.

"Well, it's up to you and the boss, of course," he conceded, to Johanna's surprise. "But if Jo feels she can put up with us I think we should grab her." He looked about the room. "No enemies about, I see. You must have got rid of the last one."

"I did," Douglas O'Malley nodded. "But I've a feeling he'll be back."

"Then let me out of here!" Shay picked up his bag. "Cats, love," he explained to Johanna. "I can't bear 'em. This place scares me rigid at times. You never know what he'll have in it. Come on, let's go find some tea. I feel like the Sahara."

He had driven up from Donegal all the way in grilling sunshine. "You'd never believe the summer they're having out there. No rain for six weeks." And certainly the car standing in the drive, its yellow sides white with dust, bore witness to this. Thrown on the back seat were tweed pieces and hanks of yarn. "And that's another day's night!" Shay groaned ruefully, turning them over. "I don't know what the boss is going to say to these, but I can make a pretty good guess."

43

# CHAPTER FIVE

THE kitchen had every conceivable item of equipment, all in gleaming white against a midnight blue and white wallpaper. In the window a black and white striped cloth covered a table to which were drawn black ladderback chairs with cane bottoms. Shay opened a cupboard and extracted cups and saucers in the same midnight blue.

"That order," Johanna asked diffidently. "Did you get it?"

"We did."

"Oh, I *am* glad. Congratulations!"

"Not mine, love," he paused to lift the kettle which had boiled. "It was sewn up by the time I got there. You remember Doug called me?" Johanna nodded. "And I'd been wondering about Felgate-Winter, why he hadn't shown up?" She nodded again. "Well, lo and behold, they'd been off playing golf together. If you ask me, the deal was closed on the nineteenth hole!"

"But it was your selling, surely, the day before," Johanna protested, conscious of a rush of tenderness similar to that day in the car park. Shay was a lot nicer than his "pop" appearance, cheeky smile, deep violet white-rolled sweater, brash way of making an entrance. Something quite unassuming now looked out from the bold eyes.

"Oh, I don't know. It may have helped. It wouldn't have done it alone. That's the thing about Doug that never ceases to amaze me. He's quite unpredictable. He was utterly browned off about having to go at all, it was only because of Myles, of course, and the bosses both being knocked up, but he went over big, Jo, believe me, he really did. Not that he talked much, mind you, that was my job." He broke off to offer her sugar. "He was the quality or the ballast or something."

It was not in the usual run of brotherly talk, but hearing it was curiously touching. "Has he a big practice?" she asked.

"Bigger than he wants really for part-time," Shay

answered. "Mornings he lectures in college." He drank thirstily and lifted the teapot.

"Shay," she dreaded the answer, but she had to ask, "were—Douglas and Myles very close?"

"Yes, very," he said impersonally, reaching for the milk jug. "That always struck me. They were as different as chalk from cheese, of course, but they got on awfully well. At home, we always said that." Again the phrasing was odd. "There was ten years between them too, but they really were—awfully close. In fact if Doug ever got his hands on . . ." he paused.

To Johanna the world seemed to have grown appreciably darker. Her hands went to her knees, gripping them. The dark blue cups and saucers and the boldly striped cloth blurred, slipped and started to spin.

"What girl?" she asked.

Shay was staring at her. "It wasn't a *girl*. It was a fellow by the name of Bourke. He got his licence endorsed. I'm talking about the crash," he added.

"Oh! Yes, of course." The picture cleared again, the swirling tide ebbed. How could she have been so foolish?

Shay, however, was still looking at her. "But I think there *was* a bird somewhere, wherever Myles was going, and I'm pretty sure Doug thinks so too. We'd both got to know the signs."

"Yes," said Johanna tightly. This was not news, no one who had ever known Myles could have been fool enough to suppose he had not had girls from the time he went to kindergarten. But hearing Shay's words implied something else and that something hurt quite sickeningly.

"I'm not pretending Myles was a saint," Shay finished. "But girls like that have a lot to answer for."

Say something, Johanna urged herself desperately, say something, even if it's only yes. Speech, however, seemed to be quite beyond her powers. The oppressive silence was broken by something else, car wheels on the gravel and the sound of brakes.

"That'll be the boss," Shay rose to peer out the window. "Oh, it's all right. Doug's there," he reported.

The car had stopped and its doors were open. Partially out of vision Douglas and another man were helping some-

45

one from the front passenger seat. She heard a voice say irritably: "All *right*. I can manage!"

"Shame about the boss. It gives him hell at times." From her side Shay volunteered the information in the same tone that she had wondered about before, sympathetic but impersonal.

"Dammit, give me a chance." The pain-fraught voice sounded again and beside her Shay's thumbs went down expressively.

"That's Mr. Baldwin. He and his wife take him out quite often," he supplied.

Baldwin! The name struck a chord, this time not hard to recall. Mrs. O'Malley's secretary, dark and willowy in the attractively woven dress, had been Geraldine Baldwin. Were these her parents? Meanwhile, the dragging footsteps sounded closer. Somewhere nearer still a door opened. Douglas' voice said something and was answered still irritably: "Yes, yes, I daresay."

Listening, Johanna tried hard to fight her feelings of dismay. Obviously, Matthew O'Malley was having a bad day, equally obviously this was what Douglas had warned her about. There should be no room for any emotion outside of pity. But there was. Standing there as the water splashed into the washing up bowl, she thought frantically: If he does give me the job will I ever cope?

She was alone. Shay had gone back to his car for something he had forgotten.

Once again, Johanna thought how strange it was that Myles had never spoken of Shay. They were so alike that they could almost have been twins, though they would never have been mistaken for each other. How old was Shay? Did he come between Douglas and Myles?

And then, imperiously and so unexpectedly that she almost dropped the cup she was drying, the telephone shrilled, so loud, so clamorous, that it could only be in the kitchen. She slewed round, saw it, fingered it timidly, and lifted the receiver.

"Will you come in, please?" the caller rasped, and put the phone back before she could utter a word.

Who was it? Where were they? Had they thought they were addressing Douglas or Shay? Once again, sense prevailed. She wanted this job, she'd begged for it and if

46

Matthew O'Malley needed something there must be no hanging back. She let the white phone back into its cradle and marched firmly into the hall.

She hadn't seen it yet, for Shay had brought her in through the back door, and now her eye took in delightedly its aqua paint, deep green carpet and kingfisher-lined alcoves. Doors opened off it and one of them was ajar. Beyond, a room with deep brown walls and shuttered windows, its floor part white tiles, part peat brown carpet. From the doorway she saw more, a long black leather settee, a brown swivel chair and, at the top of the room, almost like an altar, a gleaming white desk.

The man behind it did not look up. His head was dark, his hands very brown against the cuffs of his bitter lemon shirt. She supposed you could not judge properly while he was looking down, and yet it was always her early impressions of a person that lasted. Matthew O'Malley would always be a neat dark head, a poplin shirt and a hand, small and deeply tanned, scribbling away on a pad. It was a picture that made nonsense of those difficult halting feet.

"How is your mother? Did you give her my message?" he put the questions without looking up.

"I'm sorry, Mr. O'Malley," Johanna faltered, "I'm not Shay."

The hand stopped moving, the head jerked up. She saw the almost theatrical wings of grey in the dark hair, the slight bags under the pansy brown eyes—Shay's eyes, not Myles's, but the face, clear, small and very wide awake, was almost that of a boy. It was a boy, the boy perhaps who thirty odd years ago had come courting a redhead, who looked at her and observed in a funny shy sort of bark: "I don't think we need to be sorry about that." He followed with the query she'd anticipated. "Who are you? Should I know you?"

A man at least in the middle fifties and often in pain, he was still the handsomest of the O'Malleys. Douglas had nothing at all of him, Myles's chin had gone too rugged, Shay was the most like him, but even he had not made the precise Spanish Grandee features. It was the sort of face that would always call forth in a woman that little bit more. It did so now with her. She said breathlessly:

47

"No, but I hope you will. I'm Johanna Dykes and I'm applying for the post of your housekeeper. Your son is thinking it over."

"Douglas?"

She nodded.

"Can't see what it's got to do with him," the quick voice commented. "How old are you?"

"Twenty." She hesitated and plunged. "I know you'll think me too young, but . . ."

"On the contrary, I wouldn't change an hour of you." The dark long-lashed eyes appraised her. Not even Myles had ever looked at her quite like that, so excitingly, so challengingly.

"People are never the worse for being young," Matthew O'Malley continued in a tone that had suddenly become businesslike. "Provided they're enthusiastic and have a mind to work. Those are both qualities that tend to diminish with age. This won't be an easy post, I'm told I'm devilishly difficult, so it's no use engaging some tired old fuddy-duddy. We also," he added, "come and go at all times, at least Shay does. I can't do as much of that myself as I used to. I'm told that makes for trouble over meals. You see, I believe in putting my cards on the table, Miss Dykes, that way you have no comeback afterwards."

Johanna caught her breath. "Does that mean I can have the job?"

There was a pause and once again she found herself being studied. Then quickly, almost lightly, Matthew O'Malley replied: "Yes, all right. First thoughts anyway. We'll have another chat before you go."

She was elated. It had been so easy. She liked Matthew O'Malley and she felt he liked her too. At any rate he had accepted her offer to cook supper. Someone referred to as "Alice" would have left food in and Shay would show her where things were. She couldn't help wondering how they managed normally.

Left alone, Johanna found an apron and set to work amid an array of utensils that suggested Sheila O'Malley herself must be fond of cooking. There was nothing imaginative about straight up fried chicken, and after all this meal was in the nature of initiation. She'd simmer the chicken with onion, mix it with tomato and butter

48

and bake it in individual ring moulds. There were a dozen of these, she took out four. The mushrooms could be fried and put in the centre of the rings. For "afters" a fresh fruit salad. There wasn't time for it to stand as long as she'd like, but that couldn't be helped.

A lot to do, but the kitchen was a joy to work in and she was undisturbed. Douglas O'Malley was apparently still down in the surgery, Shay closeted with his father. In something under an hour and a half she was ready. Four plates held four rings of chicken and tomato, filled with crisp curls of mushroom and surrounded with frozen sliced beans. The fruit salad was in its dish and the coffee was perking. The question was where to serve it.

Jauntily, Johanna knocked on the door of the brown-walled room, turned its handle and went in. The white desk was strewn with the tweed she'd seen in Shay's car, Shay was holding another piece and he looked deflated.

"This is what I'm up against all the time," his father was saying tetchily. "I want something unusual. These are no use. I wouldn't let Felgate-Winter see one of them." He broke off to look at Johanna. "Yes, what is it? Is the thing on the door not working?" It was as though a cloud had come down on the velvet brown eyes and the winning smile. The face was weary and cold and so was the voice.

"The thing on the door?" Johanna faltered.

"Show her, Shay," Matthew commanded. His hand, she noticed, was pressing a switch on his desk.

Shay rose looking as weary but not at all cold. "I think it's probably supper time, sir," he said gently. "Are you ready for us, Jo?"

By now, she'd glanced backwards at the door frame and seen a small oblong panel. It contained three circles, a green one marked Enter, an amber marked Wait and a red one marked Engaged. The red one was illuminated. It stayed on. The hand, she realized, was still on the switch.

"Oh dear, I'm sorry," she said breathlessly. "But it is supper and I was just wondering where you'd like it."

"At the moment, nowhere," Matthew rasped. He turned back to the tweed as though Johanna did not exist. "This, for example. It's pathetic. Which of them dreamed it up?" He did not give Shay time to answer but ran on relentlessly, "No use mincing words. I'm disappointed.

I don't know what you said to them down there, I know if I'd been able to go myself I wouldn't have come back with stuff like this."

Nobody was even thinking about supper, nobody was even thinking about Johanna. They had left her to stand there in an agony of indecision. If she stayed, Matthew O'Malley would snap at her again, if she went, would he give her or the meal another thought? You were warned, she reminded herself, Douglas . . . Douglas! She'd almost forgotten him. He must be still in the surgery. This, however, as she approached it had a closed down look. The venetian blind with which Mark had been fiddling was straight again and all the slats were closed. She tried the door. It was locked.

She was returning dejectedly to the house when a voice hailed her:

"Hullo there. Looking for me?"

It seemed to come from above and she glanced sharply upwards. Douglas O'Malley was leaning over the balcony in the dormer storey.

She halted, craning her neck. "Yes. I—I was wondering about supper."

The face above her registered first surprise, then amusement. The left hand came up from the balcony rail to allow its owner glance at the wrist. "You have a point," he conceded judiciously. "Will you come up?"

She would have preferred that he come down, but half a loaf was better than no supper. Particularly no supper for Shay, who had had a long grilling drive with no lunch stop and was now enduring a different kind of grilling. She ran up the iron staircase to the balcony.

"*Cead mile failte,*" said her host politely.

She started.

"In other words sassenachs welcome here," he translated. "A hundred thousand welcomes."

"Thank you," she murmured uncertainly, distrusting the teasing glint which before had been directed at Mark. "Oh!" Out through the french door had padded the biggest dog she'd ever seen.

"Meet Flann," Douglas O'Malley invited. "He vets all my callers."

The giant came forward and Johanna patted its

reachy neck. "How do you do, Flann?" she asked respectfully. "You're a big fellow, aren't you?" To Flann's master she put a different query. "What is he?"

"A Great Dane," Douglas O'Malley answered. "And a great friend," he added simply. "Come in." Johanna found herself being ushered through the french door. Inside, the long bright sitting-room was a harmony of blues and golds, a wallpaper that looked like pinewood, a dark blue carpet, two converted oil lamps with globes of golden glass, curtains and covers in a dark blue material flowered in gold and turquoise.

"Make yourself at home while I go and reconnoitre," Douglas O'Malley bade her.

*Reconnoitre?* It was an odd word. "I don't like to bother you," she began nervously. "It's just that . . ."

"You were thinking about supper," he supplied, and she nodded.

"Quite understandable," he said gravely. A door was ajar at the far end of the room. He walked through it. "And what do you fancy?" he called back. "Steak and mushrooms? Omelette?"

It took a few seconds to realize that he was offering her supper. He thought that was what she'd come for.

It was too much. "Stop offering me supper!" Johanna exploded. The grey eyes widened and a murmur: "What then?" tried to make itself heard. No matter. Nothing would stop her now. "All I want is for you to come down and have yours before it's ruined!"

"H—have . . ." Douglas O'Malley was stammering. "Don't tell me you've . . ."

"I've got your supper, Mr. O'Malley," Johanna said briskly. "And your father's and Shay's. It's all ready downstairs and I can't get any of you to come and eat it. I can't even find out where you usually have it."

"Well, that's easy." Again that infuriating gleam. "Up here. What is it, by the way?"

"Chicken and tomato rings, mushrooms and beans and fruit salad," Johanna said as though hypnotized.

"Very nice too. We were just going to have herrings."

"We?" she echoed dazedly.

"Flann and I." All at once the tone changed. "I'm sorry, Johanna. I'm afraid I've been finding it an irresistible temptation seeing how big your eyes can get. But I am sorry—for a lot of things. You weren't to know that I'm not generally part of the household. Flann and I do for ourselves."

"*Three* adults . . ." Johanna began accusingly.

"Yes," he agreed. "My father, my mother and Shay. My mother's responding well, I'm happy to say. I've just been down to see her. There's a good chance she could be home in a week. That's why I put her into the advertisement." The annoying glint was back. "But wait a moment. I'm not finished apologizing. I'm sorry for appearing to forget about you. The fact is I never dreamed you were still here. It was my intention to write to you about the job."

"I've got it," Johanna struck in rashly. "I've seen your father."

The glint changed subtly. "I see. And that's why you're cooking supper?"

She nodded and began to feel unsure again. That exasperated voice and the red light on the door . . .

"And my father doesn't want to know?" the voice probed gently.

"I just didn't know what to say," she murmured.

"Don't worry," he bade her calmly. "You said and did exactly right. It's a waste of time arguing. He just comes round his own way and forgets it's not his idea. Come on, I'll show you."

Johanna following his broad back down the iron staircase was anything but convinced.

Douglas did not tap on the door of his father's room. He marched straight in, and to Johanna, following him timidly, nothing seemed to have changed. Matthew O'Malley, flicking through a file of correspondence, was saying irritably: "I should think we can forget about this order altogether. Tell Felgate-Winter these days we're only in the market for arranging our own funeral."

There was a nasty dig to the words "these days". Douglas didn't appear to notice. "Not interrupting anything, I hope?" he observed politely. "Johanna tells me supper is ready."

Now it would come, Johanna thought, and shuddered inwardly. Talk about putting your head into the lion's mouth! She caught her breath as Matthew O'Malley sent the file he had been studying skidding across the shiny white desk. "No, you're not interrupting anything. There's nothing to interrupt. Shay's brought back the biggest load of nothing I've ever seen." He glared angrily up into the eyes looking so unconcernedly down at him. "All right, get me up."

Wonderingly, Johanna perceived that the storm was over. Shay flashed her a cheerful grin. Douglas bent his weight to his father's and helped him to his feet.

"Don't tell me you're honouring us," Matthew said pantingly.

"The idea is really to claim my chicken and tomato ring," his elder son answered solemnly.

Not only was the storm over, but Johanna found it hard to believe that it had ever been. Supper was a relaxed, indeed almost a gay meal. Everyone praised her cooking, Shay told funny stories, and Matthew barked out several unexpected witticisms. As he ate, the deadness left his skin and it glowed warmly apricot. Studying covertly the small-featured oval face and the smile of first-degree charm, Johanna wondered again whether any of his forebears could have been Spanish. He looked barely old enough to have a son of twenty-two. That Douglas, bulky and with those few flecks of grey, should also be his son was little short of incredible. He and Sheila must have married very young, and what a pair they must have made. Still did, in fact, and it was touching to recall that his first greeting to-day, when he'd assumed that she was Shay, had been a question about his wife: "How is your mother? Did you give her my message?"

And that reminded her. "I was so pleased," she said, leaning towards Shay, "to hear that your mother may soon be out of the nursing home."

It had an effect she had not anticipated. What had been a lull in the conversation froze to a deathly silence. Shay, who had had a clove of orange on his fork, seemed to have difficulty in swallowing, Douglas, on the other hand, did swallow, once and rapidly. Matthew set down his glass with a chink.

"What about Maire? What's wrong? No one told me." His dark eyes darted from one son to the other.

Douglas was the first to recover his breath. Shay was not only staring, he had flushed like a beetroot.

"It's all right, Father," Douglas said. "Maire's not ill. It's just—" he smiled. "That name again!"

"Name?" Johanna stuttered.

"Shay and I are not brothers," he told her.

"*Brothers!*" Matthew O'Malley ejaculated. "Good grief, of course you're not brothers." As the words died he looked accusingly at Johanna.

Just another small thing in the maelstrom—not brothers, but both O'Malleys. Who then was Shay? Why had he flushed so deeply? Why did Matthew appear so incensed?

"What could possibly give you that idea?" Matthew added now, in a short tone.

"Be fair, Father," Douglas broke in. "It's a very natural mistake." He turned to Johanna. "The name, I suppose. You're not the first person it's misled."

"I'm no relation," Shay was saying now. "Honestly."

"Well," Douglas corrected pedantically, "we never quite sorted that out, did we? Forty-first cousin or something like that. All the O'Malleys round Carrickdoo are more or less related."

"But you're so like . . ." Horrorstruck, Johanna bit back the words. The first pitfall and she'd walked straight into it. She wasn't supposed to know what Myles had looked like. Heaven knows she'd warned herself about it often enough. "Well—so like Mr. O'Malley," she corrected herself.

"Like me?" The voice came gratingly from the top of the table. "Why should he be like me? We're not related."

"No, I know, it was just a thought." Her mistake had been embarrassing enough. The finishing touch was the flush that had now risen in Matthew O'Malley's cheekbones. She didn't want to look at it or at him, but she couldn't take her eyes away.

It helped not at all that two other thoughts had suddenly assailed her. Was "Maire" Shay's mother? If so, then presumably that first question this afternoon had referred to her.

The last mouthfuls of the meal were taken with a noticeable ebb of gaiety. No one said anything about

54

Sheila O'Malley's imminent discharge from the nursing home and, more disconcerting to Johanna, Matthew O'Malley also omitted to refer again to the housekeeping job. It seemed she must herself take the initiative.

"Will it be all right then for me to start tomorrow or Monday?" As an approach it lacked finesse and she was dismayed to see Matthew O'Malley's brows draw together.

"I'm sorry, Miss Dykes, I can't be rushed on this. It's an important decision." The tone made her feel that she'd been presumptuous.

"I'm sorry." She flushed. "I thought you . . ."

"They were first thoughts only. I told you that," Matthew O'Malley pointed out. "Leave your address and I'll let you know."

Just the pattern Shay had predicted. He was going to discuss her with Douglas and Douglas, his own misgivings now backed by the supper episode, would naturally turn his thumbs down. So much for the great plan. Shay, the one person who would welcome her, was not in the family at all. And more than that, he who'd given her the idea of making reparation was the one to whom she owed nothing. It was surely the oddest caprice.

Now she looked at him. He had carried the tray into the kitchen and was stacking the dishes. "How often do the buses run? I should be getting back."

"Oh, not yet," he said easily. "And anyway, I'll drive you."

"I think I should go now." Johanna would have been hard put to it to explain in words why. A feeling of shame perhaps for the thought that that young saucy face between the dark sideboards could make a person live again.

"Did I ever tell you about the Irishman and the Scotsman?" Shay asked.

"No!"

"Then don't you think I should?"

"No!" she laughed.

"Please." His arm had gone round her, young and strong, like Myles's arm; his temple nuzzled hers.

"Not interrupting anything, I hope?" came a quiet voice. Douglas O'Malley was standing in the kitchen.

To Johanna, flushed and trying to extricate herself, it seemed for a second that she'd been caught in an act of the rankest treachery. Myles's fiancée consoling herself not a month after his death! She even wondered why the grey eyes surveying them were not accusing and contemptuous instead of, as undoubtedly they were, kind and condoning. But of course Douglas O'Malley didn't know her secret. To him she was just a student looking for a holiday job. And Shay was someone who worked hard for little thanks, someone about whom he "often had a conscience." Nevertheless, she tried to slip from Shay's embrace. Unsuccessfully. He was cheerful and unabashed.

"You darned well are!" he retorted.

"You know," Douglas O'Malley remarked conversationally, "I was just thinking how times have changed. When I was young," lines of amusement creased his face, "I never asked my favours at the kitchen sink. If I couldn't get hold of a moon I got a mountain. Well, go on, what are you waiting for?" he added briskly. "I'll do these." Already he was stripping off his jacket.

The word "money" could have summed up Knockbeg, its kitchen equipment, its hall with the silk-lined alcoves, Matthew O'Malley's room with its brown hessian-covered walls, the dining-room with its floor-length white curtains against vermilion red walls and the beautifully carved pale furniture. And now a garden as opulent and as contemporary. The striped velvet lawns swept down to a kidney-shaped swimming pool, turquoise blue, with steps and changing pavilion of honey-coloured cut stone.

Johanna thought for a moment what it would have been like to have come here as Myles's bride, and as though he'd read her thoughts, Shay said: "No one uses the pool much now. It was really for Myles. He used to go in every evening as soon as he got home from work."

"What about you?" she asked.

"Oh yes. When I've time. There's not much superfluity of that." He went on to explain that he had been based in Donegal as Assistant Works Manager until Myles's accident, but following this Matthew O'Malley had invited him to move up to Dublin and live in Knockbeg so as to be on hand.

"In other words, work a twenty-four-hour day," Johanna opined.

"Well, I've not exactly been the loser," Shay pointed

out loyally. "And I'm with him all the way when he says things would be different if he could get around himself. They would, believe you me. He's dynamic, or used to be. And besides, one way and another, my family owes him a lot." He looked as though he wanted to say more and changed his mind. "My grandfather has worked for O'Malley tweeds for fifty years. He taught me all I know about weaving. He's a great old lad, Jo. I'd like you to meet him."

"I'd love to, Shay," Johanna said warmly. "I'd love to go to Donegal."

"I wonder . . ." Shay pursed his lips. "Must you go back to England?"

"Oh yes. If I don't get this job." She wouldn't try for another, it would be pointless now. "My parents didn't really want me to come to Ireland."

The dark eyes considered her. "Just your parents?"

Johanna looked back at them. "Yes."

"But you're such a doll, Jo, there must be—someone." He paused.

"Yes. He died," she said breathlessly.

"Oh!" Warm sympathy charged the brown eyes. "I'm sorry, love. I didn't understand." In the lengthening shadows his puckish face was contrite. "Back there, you must have been praying for me."

In such a nebulous situation no words could be trusted. She shook her head. One point only had been reached. His warmth, his arms, his absurdities had not hurt, they had gladdened. And now, she thought, he would again say something crazy, produce another not very funny story, anything to cheer her up. He was so young—and so sweet. But when Shay said softly: "Jo," the tone was so different from her expectations that she stared.

"I'd like to level with you," he went on. "I've had a bit of that too." "So young," she'd thought. This was no young face. With the fun and the warmth wiped off it, it was sharp and mature. And he was so still that he might have been a statue on a plinth.

"Did she—die?"

"No. She just made it very plain that I was wasting my time," he answered curtly. "Oh, I don't blame her. I must have been mad."

He might not blame her, Johanna thought, watching the face that had changed so astonishingly, but he'd been badly hurt and the wounds had not yet closed. Somehow it changed things. She had under-estimated Shay, seen him as someone sweet but not very deep. Now with a strange quickening of her own pulses she seemed to be looking at a new person.

"Hullo. Is this where you are?" Douglas O'Malley had a way of asking unnecessary questions. He had loomed up unnoticed, Flann at his heels, and now he seated himself on the bench at a right angle to Shay. Hardly the leprechaun type; his posture of legs apart and elbows on knees made him look squarer than ever.

"Aren't you going to ask if you're interrupting anything?" Shay enquired hopefully, and pushed his back against the broad shoulder.

"All right, I can take a hint," Douglas replied. "*And* give one." With as little effort as when he'd lifted his father out of the chair he used his same shoulder as a battering ram.

Shay slithered along the bench. "I thought you were going out!" he yelped aggrievedly.

"Yes, but I have her trained," Douglas answered. "She calls for me now."

Was he joking? Did the mighty Douglas really go in for dating? Johanna weighing it in her mind, realized abruptly that he was looking at her.

"It's you I really came to find. A message from my father. The job's yours if you still want it and he'll be glad if you could come in tomorrow afternoon."

She couldn't believe it. Her hopes had gone so low. "Oh yes," she gasped. "And thank you."

"Me?" The brows lifted.

"I thought you might have put in a word for me," she said hesitantly.

"Did you now?" He surveyed her consideringly. "You could be right at that. Doubtless I need my head examined."

"There's Gerry," Shay interrupted. "On the terrace, look!" He pointed.

A girl, dark and willowy, in a cream dress, its matching jacket slung across her shoulders, was descending the brick steps to the lawn. She waved and Douglas waved back and went to meet her. Johanna, grappling amazedly with the realization that the date not only existed but was the super-charged Geraldine Baldwin in person, watched as the two figures approached each other. Geraldine, light on her feet, came swiftly; Douglas walked on his heels and looked sturdier than ever.

It was again a surprise and not a particularly welcome one that they should both come back to the swimming pool.

"You two might as well know each other now as later," Douglas said smoothly. "Geraldine, this is Johanna Dykes who's going to stoke the home fires for the next few weeks. Johanna, this is Geraldine Baldwin without whom O'Malley Tweeds would undoubtedly fall to bits."

Johanna felt she ought to rise and did so. Shay had already untelescoped his long legs and greeted the arrival with a nod. "Hullo, Gerry, how's tricks?" He had flushed, but Johanna only noticed this in passing. She was herself too agonizedly conscious of the eyes that were fixed on her. Geraldine Baldwin had remarkable eyes, violet blue, veined like a flower and amused. A mere second sufficed them to take stock.

"How are you, Miss Dykes?" A long-fingered hand, the wrist encircled by a chunky gold bracelet, touched Johanna's. "So sorry I wasn't able to do anything for you. We had no car going up." She glanced laughingly at Douglas, who was frowning in puzzlement. "All right, Doug, I haven't gone mad. We've met before. Miss Dykes was in the office—Tuesday, was it?—yes, the day before your mother collapsed."

It was said so pleasantly that to suspect a double meaning seemed ludicrous. Or was it? Johanna asked herself. The words, light as they were, could contain an implication both damning and terrifying.

Evidently someone else thought so too. "Well, don't say it as though Johanna were responsible for that!" Douglas derided gently.

He was looking, Johanna realized, straight into her hot little face. There were no mirrors round the swimming pool, but from the fire in her cheeks Johanna knew exactly how she must look, poppy face, saucer eyes, fat little falling lip. Someone who'd been caught stealing the jam. Because as yet she had not told Douglas O'Malley anything about her call at O'Malley House. She'd hoped to leave it until she felt more sure of her ground.

"You've met my mother, then?"

"Yes," she jerked. "Miss Baldwin was out when I called, so she saw me." Now of course there would be questions. She'd been evasive and Douglas O'Malley was so aggressively straightforward that she could guess his reaction. It came and left her blinking with astonishment.

"Oh yes? That would have been when you thought of the project on tweed?"

She nodded breathlessly.

"Any good?" he questioned.

Her eyes widened.

"My mother," he elucidated. "Could she cope in the absence of big brass?" The head had gone to one side, the face was droll.

"You know that wasn't what I meant," Johanna began, faint with relief.

"All right," he agreed, laughing. "See you tomorrow. Shay will pick you up around four. Geraldine, my dear," he added, "if you want to catch that thing at nine-five we shall have to run for it." A hand went chummily under Geraldine's elbow.

"Good-bye, Mr. O'Malley, and thank you," Johanna said gratefully. "Good-bye, Miss Baldwin."

Once more the violet eyes focused themselves on her. "Oh, make it Geraldine," their owner invited with charm. "And remember, if I can help at all, I know Knockbeg nearly as well as O'Malley House.' She smiled as Douglas hustled her across the lawn.

CHAPTER SIX

"I HOPE you're wise, that's all," Pat in Reception observed next day as she handed Johanna her receipted account. "Watch out for the mountain wolves!"

"One's due in a minute," Johanna promised gaily. It was just four o clock and she was waiting for Shay. "Watch out for a yellow car.'

"This I must see." Pat glanced eagerly through her window. "No joy. There's a whacking great green one, though, just pulling up. Any use?"

"No. Must be yellow," Johanna returned, and waltzed over to the postcard stand. She felt ridiculously light-hearted, had done from the moment of waking.

"Tell me about the wolves," Pat commanded.

"Any time!" It was a silly conversation, but again she felt like being silly. "First there's wolf number one, king and slayer in chief. What he must have been like before he got arthritis I tremble to think. Then there's my wolf, nearly as dishy, but he's just a sheep in wolf's clothing, and then there's the middle one who doesn't look like a wolf at all so we'll call him the wolf in sheep's clothing." To be received in complete silence was surprising, for after all Pat had asked. "So what advice for Little Red Riding Hood?" she demanded, and swung round.

Behind the counter, Pat was gazing at her, apparently transfixed. Nearer and also gazing with level dark grey eyes was a man's trunky form. First reaction was disbelief. It wasn't possible. Her eyes were playing tricks. She blinked them and looked again. No mistake this time; Douglas O'Malley, dour as a mountain crag, was really standing there.

"I take it you're ready," he said in a tone devoid of expression.

Absurdity of absurdities, her second reaction—that the dark grey Harris tweed jacket and the black roll-neck sweater together gave quite a wolfish effect. "I thought—Shay—" she jerked.

"Playing football." He had picked up her case and was holding the hotel door open. With a despairing glance at Pat, Johanna hurried through it. The "whacking great car", an olive green outsize in station wagons, was parked at the kerb. He opened its door and she got in. If instead the ground could have opened and swallowed her she would have been grateful.

That it was the first time in weeks she'd felt light enough to act crazily could naturally not be offered in defence. She sat red-faced and hot with mortification as the long wide monster cut through the city streets. Not till these had given way to suburban roads with yester-day's mountains on the skyline did Douglas O'Malley speak.

He said quietly: "I think we need to have another talk about this job."

It sounded like a death knell. "I realize what you must have thought, Mr. O'Malley," Johanna said guiltily. "I'm sorry. I don't know what came over me."

"Your age." The gentle tone astonished her. "At twenty one ought to be able to laugh." The keenness of the accompanying look was as astonishing, it was almost as though he knew about those weeks of anguish. "It's not that I can't take a joke, even though I may look like a sheep." Desperately, she opened her mouth, but there was no chance of speaking. "But this job is not a joke," the quiet voice went on. "And we have problems enough, all of us, without having to pick up your pieces."

"Do I look as though you'd have to?" Johanna challenged, nettled.

"Frankly, yes," he answered, and drew in to give room to a following car.

Fair, if deflating, comment, and a frightening verdict on what first loving Myles and then losing him had done to her in the past four months. Before then, on balance, she'd always had in her more of her hard-headed father than her light-hearted mother. "I've said I'm sorry, Mr. O'Malley," she said soberly, "I can't help the way I look, but I promise you won't have cause to complain again of the way I behave."

It was meant sincerely, but something in the way he was regarding her made her feel that she'd said the wrong thing. The strong features looked almost regretful.

"Heavens, child," he said impatiently. She sensed oddly that the impatience was with himself. "I'm not complaining. I see enough of young things to dislike quenching them. I hate to see pekes being carried."

She laughed. She couldn't help it. "It's the first time I've ever been called a peke!"

It hurt that he did not even smile. "Johanna, please let me finish. This is very important." The hint of reproof once more caused her cheeks to tingle. "For the natural reasons, and for reasons that need not concern you, my brother's death has been a body bl w to my parents. Losing him has caused a lot of things to topple. None of this, of course, should be your concern." He little knew, she thought, stifling a shudder. "I'm telling you because when I advertised this job I thought some uninvolved third party could help them over this patch."

A bill she certainly didn't fill. Uninvolved! She was an unlit fuse. And then she heard: "It's because you're not that that I have to warn you."

"Not what?" she gasped sharply.

"Uninvolved." Had he really said it? And so matter-of-factly, his eyes on the road.

"What do you mean?" It was a thread of sound.

"What you told me yourself." He glanced casually round. "That you answered my advertisement because you'd heard about Myles and wanted to help."

Johanna closed her eyes. "Oh—that."

"It's hardly trivial. In fact it's why I thought you should be given the chance."

There was a momentary pause. The fire ebbed from her face. She thought wildly: "It's all right. He hasn't guessed," and then more calmly: "Well, how could he? I must have been mad."

"The thing is," he was appending, "you've had a curtain-raiser, as it were. My father is demanding and changeable, mostly he's in pain. My mother keeps her grief locked up to fester. Shay copes wonderfully with my father, Geraldine magnificently with my mother. Do you still want to join the team?"

She didn't really need to, but she took a second to frame it—mature, responsible, absolutely no chinks, a soldier always at the ready.

"Yes, Mr. O'Malley, yes, I do."

The grey eyes flickered. "Good," their owner said.

He went on, after glancing at his watch, to say that he had a call to make and proposed to do so on the way home. "It's up in Glenasmole. You'll probably enjoy the scenery."

It was an understatement. Once out of Rathnasee and climbing into the heart of the hills, each mile brought fresh enchantment, groves of beech and chestnut, old stone bridges, high fir-clad ridges. As far as the eye could see the mountains stood shoulder to shoulder, olive and apple green with brown butterfly shadows.

Heading towards Kilmashogue again but not too far from Glenasmole they turned along a tree-hung road at last.

"We'll be passing the Baldwin's place in a minute," Douglas O'Malley remarked, and a moment later his hand on the horn gave a vociferous salute to a creeper-covered house on the right.

"Sorry, that's just to say back soon," he explained as Johanna started. "They're expecting me for supper."

No light flashed when Johanna, mindful of yesterday's lesson, tapped decorously on Matthew O'Malley's door. Instead his voice called informally: "All right, come in."

"Look here, I'm not going to call you Miss Dykes. I hate that sort of thing. Johanna, if that's all right." The boy's smile, starting shyly which added to its charm, flashed upon her.

It was a good day. He got to his feet unaided and used only one stick to get to the terrace where Johanna served and shared his afternoon tea. Shay was still out and Douglas had gone to his flat to change.

"We don't see much of him, you know. He fends for himself," Matthew confided. "I hope he's found time to show you your room."

"Yes, it's delightful." She'd adored it on sight, notching up as another tribute to Sheila O'Malley its apple green walls, sage green carpet, white built-in furniture, green and white curtains and the white lace bedcover.

"And to put you in the picture about how we do things here?" was the next question. Surprising as it seemed, Matthew O'Malley took the running of Knockbeg as seriously as the affairs of his business. He went over it in such detail that Johanna's head began to buzz. It was a relief when the recital was interrupted by a caller, Harry Blake, who had been in O'Malley House last week.

"Organize some supper for us later on," Matthew O'Malley said as Johanna left them together. "No hurry. Whenever you like."

Hard on Harry's heels came Shay's yellow car. "Jo!"

The driver, this time in a white sweater, jumped out and took her hand. "Sorry about this afternoon. They were a man short. Everything all right?"

With Douglas there might be the occasional moment of closeness. With Shay, she realized warmly, you had it all the time. And to-day he, like his employer, seemed quite untroubled by circumstances.

"Someone is with Mr. O'Malley," Johanna explained, and Shay glanced at the car and said: "Yes. Harry Blake. More lines on the weather map. Let's scarper." Harry Blake, he exemplified, leading her down the steps to the lawn, was chief designer at O'Malley Tweeds and had doubtless been summoned for further discussions on yesterday's samples.

"But it's Sunday," Johanna began.

"When you know Matt better, my love, you won't be surprised if he sends for you at two o'clock in the morning."

"It should be—very!" Johanna said decisively.

"Well, maybe," Shay allowed. "But it happens quite frequently to me. He doesn't sleep well, you see, and sometimes he gets an idea." Without warning he stopped and stripped off his sweater, revealing a pair of shoulders the colour of walnut juice and a chest, as brown, and hairless as a child's. Johanna, about to voice her disapproval of Matthew O'Malley's methods, was halted by the realization that her escort was unfastening his jeans.

*"Don't mind me "* she squeaked.

"No, pet. Don't intend to," he grinned, and stepped free, to stand before her in a pair of swimming trunks. "Coming in?"

If she could have been sure Matthew O'Malley would not call her with further instructions she would have been tempted. As things were she declined. Shay's slim form, arms outstretched and down-pointing, took a long spaced header into the turquoise pool, coming up to swim its length as rhythmically as a speed boat. He did this three or four times, then he pulled himself up the aluminium ladder, fetched a towel from the pavilion and sat down beside Johanna.

It seemed the most natural thing in the world to take the towel and rub his hair dry, hair thick and black as

Myles's hair had been but straight where the other had waved.

"You're thin," she said maternally.

"And you're nice," Shay returned softly. "Very, very nice."

Unwonted gravity wiped the urchin look from his face. She wondered if this was the way it had looked to the girl who had turned him down, the mouth more sensitive than she'd realized, and the chin clefted as Myles's chin had been. He leaned a little forward as though he were going to kiss her.

That was not like Myles, because Myles wouldn't have hesitated. He'd been like a fever in the blood, exciting, devil-may-care. Shay's devilry was as innocent as a child doing imitations. His true Credo was a man, a woman, a baby, a home, and the same face on the pillow year after year. They were the things her parents had had, the things that had prompted that fateful telephone call from Norwich.

The same face on the pillow year after year . . . and suddenly a thought whirled in upon her making her catch her breath.

When she'd steadied again Shay had taken the towel from her and was drying his ears. "I haven't ordered yet, have I?" he quipped. "One horse, please, whole and medium rare!" The urchin mask was back. Whoever he'd seen during that grave moment he was now seeing her again, little Jo, nice kid but coming to bits so easily and having to be put together again . . .

Well, before this household was much older it was going to realize that little Jo was every bit as mature and responsible as—well, Geraldine Baldwin.

Harry Blake stayed to supper and at the coffee stage they talked shop. Matthew O'Malley had come round to a less morbid view of the Felgate-Winter order. He was not going to opt out. On the contrary it had turned overnight into the ideal vehicle for what he termed "Young O'Malley". Johanna remembered the name. Harry Blake had used it in Sheila O'Malley's office.

"Do you think Felgate-Winter will play along, sir?" Shay asked doubtfully. "They have their own brand name, you know."

"If he gets the right sell of course he'll play," his employer returned. "And that's up to you. Shouldn't have the slightest difficulty," he added. "With the coverage we're giving it, 'Young O'Malley' will soon be a household word. If Felgate-Winter or anyone else can say: 'In a Young O'Malley handweave exclusive to so-and-so,' he's got a sales boost for free. He's no fool. He'll see that."

"Young O'Malley" began to be less of a question mark. It was obviously also a brand name and part of a sales campaign to capture the young market. Designers and department stores were doing this in ever-increasing numbers.

"And now that you are here, Harry," Matthew continued, "what's the report from Pearson? Are you keeping on his tail?"

Harry Blake, to Johanna's concern, tipping cigarette ash into his beautiful Wedgwood saucer, said a completely non-committal: "Oh yes, Matt, I am."

"This chap Pearson." To Johanna's surprise she found herself being addressed. "Supposed to be coming up with a house style for packaging and stationery. You should see the fee he asked. I haven't had a blink out of him. Nor out of Richardson. Ask *him* to come and see me, Shay. He was finding out about television too. I'm interested in that."

"I'll ring him tomorrow, sir," Shay promised.

Johanna, watching Harry Blake, thought she had seldom seen anyone look so uneasy.

"We're pressed to use these people," Matthew said testily. "Supposed to do the world and all. Far as I can see they do nothing. Look here, get me Pearson now. Let me talk to him. And get me Richardson too. The press release should have been out days ago."

Johanna watched pityingly as the small sunburned hands gripped the table edge. If Matthew O'Malley had been old, even if he had looked his age, it might not have been so tragic, but the slight handsome body that could no longer fulfil the demands made on it was just that.

"*One* paralytic snail round here is enough," Matthew panted, and Shay caught Johanna's eyes and grinned admiringly.

Harry Blake, however, looked more disapproving than compassionate.

"You can't ring them now, Matt. It's Sunday."

"I don't care what day it is." The hands and the taut arms, to-day sleeved in baby pink batiste, had done their work and Matthew O'Malley was on his feet. "So long as it gets me action."

"Careful, sir." Shay touched his arm supportingly.

"Yes, Matt, easy does it." Harry's face was also suffused with anxiety. "I—er—" he hesitated. "Fact is, it's not their fault. Sheila told them both to hold off."

"*To hold off?*" The words were a stutter of disbelief and for a second it seemed that the speaker had no words. But in the next he was himself again, shoating questions. "Why wasn't I told about this? Did you know?" The dark eyes smouldering under the beetle brows were directed at Shay.

"No, not a word," Shay said at once, but with a flush that caused Johanna to wonder. If he were not implicated there was surely no need to look guilty.

Anyway it was no place for her. Shay was Matthew's personal assistant, Harry Blake as well as O.C. Designs was plainly an old friend, she was the newest of employees. Besides, she was scared. Knockbeg had echoes of one tragedy; that tragedy of another kind should also stalk it was a great deal more than she'd bargained for. Yet in that oblique way of his Douglas had warned her of it. Myles's death, he had said, had caused a lot of things to topple. But oh, it was horrible. This lovely home and the man and woman who owned it, each with their startling good looks, and underneath . . . she shivered, knocking the cups she was piling.

"And when did my charming wife do all this?" Matthew O'Malley was asking, his voice now icy cold.

"Tuesday morning," Harry Blake answered. "I told her it was a mistake, but—don't be too hard on her, Matt. She wasn't herself. It was the day before she went into hospital.'

Johanna, putting the percolator on to the tray, found herself almost praying that the appeal would strike home. That day Sheila O'Malley had certainly not been herself. Everything about her had pointed to intolerable strain.

She found herself willing Matthew desperately to understand; death shouldn't be a divider, when her own parents had lost a child it had made them even closer.

But now Matthew O'Malley's voice cut once again into the troubled silence: "Then all I can say is the longer she stays there the better!"

"Never a dull moment!" Shay's face, brash and gamin again, came round the kitchen door.

The levity grated. Johanna was still seeing Sheila O'Malley's tortured eyes and Matthew's gnarled knuckles. It had been horrible. She couldn't laugh. She said so.

"Laugh or go mad, I've learned that," Shay returned.

"He said the longer she was ill the better. You couldn't laugh about that. It was wicked."

"She did him a pretty wicked turn."

The tone gave Johanna her bearings. "You're on his side, aren't you?"

"Yes. All the way. He may change his mind a bit and he may lash out—he's got plenty to make him, he carries the whole bang lot. And anyway none of it lasts. He's not bad-tempered basically, and he just couldn't be bothered being spiteful. I respect him, I like him, and I speak his language." To Johanna's embarrassment a flush once again crept through his face.

Matthew O'Malley had flushed like that when she'd commented on Shay's likeness to him. And just after he had enquired so peremptorily for "Maire" who was Shay's mother. No! It was now her own turn to flush. There were enough dark places in this household without her dreaming up some more.

"So what is Young O'Malley, then?" she asked.

"In one word," Shay answered, "it's Myles." The whole scheme was to have been Myles's baby; the designs would have been his and all publicity material carry his photograph, labels and packaging reproducing this as a cartoon figure. There had been talk of a new van painted in Young O'Malley symbols. "It's a money-spinner," Shay finished.

"*Is?*" Johanna queried.

"*Is.* The boss won't budge on this one, Jo. It's too big." Shay's face had changed again, this time to shrewd-

69

ness, the face perhaps that had won him his present position. And still uncannily like Matthew's, Matthew who would ride rough-shod over his wife's grief.

"It's cruel, Shay. She couldn't stand it. She loved him so much."

The face between the sideboards looked suddenly wise. "You're very sweet, darling, but if that's your idea of love it's not mine." He seemed about to say more when the house phone buzzed. Johanna, who could never remember that this was likely to happen, jumped. Shay stretched across and lifted it. "Right, sir, coming," he said crisply, and was gone.

There was no sign of him returning when she had finished washing up, so she went out. Somehow Knockbeg had become obnoxious, a house where people hated each other and those who were otherwise good friends found themselves on opposite sides. A few hours ago with the coffee perking and the table looking nice and the old grey cat rubbing against her, the house had answered something inside her; it had seemed like a home.

Now as she walked swiftly away from it, it seemed to menace her like shapes in a fog. This, after all, *was* a black glen, but Myles had controlled it, just by being there, a link between two people who seemed to loathe each other. She had helped to remove Myles and now there was no knowing what might happen.

The simple grief she had come prepared for, the compound one, terrified her.

From the shadows behind her a cold nose touched her hand and as she jumped Flann's long lithe body, blue as the dusk itself, pressed heavily against her. At the same moment Douglas's voice hailed her: "Hullo. Shay was wondering about you." In the half light, his face was a pale oval above a wall-like chest.

"Oh?" She cursed the tremble in her voice.

"Yes. I think he was afraid that like good cooks go you'd gone!" The mouth twisted into an O of amusement, but the eyes were very alert.

"Sorry," she said firmly. "I felt like a breath of air and I didnt' like to interrupt the meeting, so I just came out."

No mistaking the gleam of relief—or could it be approval—in the face regarding her.

"Going up?" he jerked his head at the winding road and the sign on which she could just make out the words No Through Road. "Or have you had enough? Right. Let's go home then," he suggested as she nodded.

Had it been Shay's slim-waisted form beside her his hand would certainly have been on her shoulder or through her arm. Douglas walked doggedly with both hands in his pockets. He was the most uninvolved person she had ever met, and yet he made the household his care and she was a part of it now and had to be brought in like a straying sheep.

At the low wall, which in daytime commanded the green plateau, her warder stopped. Ahead in the dip towards Rathnasee and Dublin City myriads of lights were twinkling. "Out there," he said, pointing, "Absolutely in a straight line, see it? That's the airport."

She found the lights and memorized them. Perhaps she could see them also from Knockbeg. The thought was comforting.

"If you feel like running in next door for a cup of sugar," Douglas's quiet voice appended.

"It's funny. I never really thought of being so near." Ireland had always seemed much farther away and an unknown quantity.

"Just a stone's throw," Douglas O'Malley commented, and added poker-faced: "Which is of course how we lost the Isle of Man." The giant, Finn Ma Cool, he told her, had one day taken up a clod of earth to fling at England, but halfway across it had fallen into the sea. "If you don't believe me you can go and see the hole where it came from. The name they have on it these days is Lough Neagh."

He looked at her for a second, his face still blanched by the rising moon, his hair flapping on his forehead, his eyes cool but kind.

"If it wasn't exactly good clean fun it wasn't as bad as it looked either. Most things aren't. I know you were upset tonight, Jo, Shay told me. I'm sorry you came in for it so soon, but don't take too much notice. You'd be surprised how it usually works out."

## CHAPTER SEVEN

ALICE, the daily help, arrived next morning and ten minutes after Douglas O'Malley had introduced them Johanna knew that here was a character. When the house phone rang Alice stumped off to answer the hall door. "Does she not recognize it?" Johanna asked, and Douglas chuckled: "Of course she does. That's a protest. She can't sit down in Trafalgar Square, so she does it this way."

Johanna wondered why the O'Malleys kept Alice, and when that evening Douglas's car passed her on the road and stopped to give her a lift she ventured to hint as much.

"Good heavens, we'd be lost without Alice!" he exclaimed reprovingly. "She'd lie down and die for my mother." He looked searchingly into his passenger's face. "Well, how was it?"

Actually, it had been quite smooth. Alice worked as well as slandering and Johanna had enojyed having someone to talk to.

Next day Shay had to leave early for Carrickdoo, so she got up early to make his breakfast and see him off. Standing beside the car on the sunny driveway, he looked at her with disarming earnestness:

"Jo love, I really appreciate this. This place a few weeks ago—anyone could have had my share of it. Now—I don't know—suddenly it seems like home."

Before she'd properly realized his intention, his arm had slid across the peacock blue cotton of her bib and brace skirt and its crisp checked shirt and drew her close —this time with a difference. The tearaway smile was gone, the laughing mouth with the square very white teeth softened and met hers.

"That guy you told me about," he said softly when it was over. "I don't know his name, but if I were where he is right now I'd be breaking just about my thousandth harp over St. Peter's head!"

His yellow car had zoomed down the drive when Johanna looked up. Douglas O'Malley was descending his iron staircase. He waved at her and went on into the house.

The day was uneventful, and to compensate the flat note struck by Shay's absence she took special pains over dinner, pork chops baked with rings of pineapple and served with soured cream. The afternoon post brought her first letter from home. Her mother appreciated all that Jo had told her about the family's health troubles, but she did hope that it would not mean Jo working all through the summer. The weather had turned wet and they were worried about the harvest. She ended with a joke. The magpies, all seven of them, were still around. "So that means the secret's still in the air, but I haven't found it out yet!" To Johanna the exclamation mark had an accusing air and heightened her guilt over not mentioning her employer's name and taking advantage of the fact that Myles's home address had never been mentioned in her parent's hearing.

The next day, however, did not look like being uneventful. Johanna was having her breakfast when Douglas O'Malley walked into the kitchen and said that his father would not require any. "Just a cup of tea. If you've got it handy I'll take it in to him."

"Oh dear!" She looked scaredly into the impassive face. "Is it a bad day?"

"Night," he corrected. She glanced again.

"I said it had been a bad night," he repeated. "I gather he's been eating pork and pineapples and cream. Oh, I know he should have had more sense, he knows he can't digest rich food the way he used to, but honestly, Jo, I think *you* might use a bit of savvy too."

"I'm most terribly sorry," she murmured. "Is there anything I can do?"

"Not now. But for heaven's sake watch it again," he bade her irritably. "This only makes trouble for everyone."

"Don't mind him, ducky," Alice consoled. "Nor him in there either." She nodded indignantly at Matthew's door. "It's always the woman's fault. Throwbacks to Adam, every one of them, if you ask me."

Notwithstanding this, when her usual time for departure arrived, she showed no sign of going. Johanna,

73

still considerably in awe of Alice, forbore to comment, Douglas, walking in at three o'clock, did so and was promptly shot down.

"It's me own time I'm in now, Mr. Douglas. I suppose I can do what I like with it.

"Ask him would he fancy a sup o'tea. I could do it for him afore I go," she called casually as Douglas approached his father's room, and when the offer was taken up Johanna was not allowed to have any part in it. "All right, ducky, I know the way he likes it." She whipped out the loaf. "I'm putting a nice bit of thin bread with it, Mr. Douglas. See will he take it."

So much for the vituperations! Alice, Johanna realized amusedly, was after all very fond of her employers.

And Matthew O'Malley was no moaner. Though still looking fragile, when she went in to remove the tea-tray he waved away all her attempts at apology. "All right, no harm done. Know better the next time—both of us."

"We know you're a good cook," Douglas O'Malley remarked as she re-entered the kitchen. "There's really no need to show off."

*Show off?* She stopped, blinking, unable to credit her ears. *Show off?* The man was insufferable! She'd like to see him produce the meals she had, all in the space of six days, in an unfamiliar kitchen and with just the cookery book she'd bought last Sunday morning to aid. The trouble she'd taken too, particularly over sauces and garnishings, home-made tomato sauce, wine sauce, chopped parsley, watercress, sour cream, things she felt bound the O'Malley family did not get every day of the week.

Show off indeed! She checked. After all, wasn't it true? All those years ago the invalid Gramps Dykes had been served nothing but the plainest and most bland of diets.

"I'm sorry," she said meekly. "It won't happen again."

"What's on for tonight?" he asked.

She'd been careful in advance—fillets of sole. Matthew's was going to be steamed, her own and Shay's fried in butter with bananas and lemon juice. "Will you join us?" she invited, and for a moment seemed to hear again, quite absurdly, an echo of that song about the rain. So silly. So silly to want this completely self-sufficient

74

man to come in anywhere. He did not need a "hideaway," and if he did he had one already, that pleasant creeper-covered house near Glenasmole.

Douglas O'Malley glanced at his watch, seemed to hesitate and shook his head. "No, thanks all the same. I've a lot of calls to make."

Matthew did not get up for dinner, though he was well enough to enjoy a modest portion. Shay and Johanna dined alone.

Shay took the indisposition lightly. "Don't worry, love. He won't hold it against you. Probably thinks it was worth it. He's quite a one for cuisine."

His own affairs occupied him more. He had not had time to get out owing to union troubles in the factory. Nothing serious, he said blithely, O'Malleys had a good record as employers and things had never got to a stoppage, not even an unofficial one. But he'd had to spend time both yesterday and to-day in meeting the various spokesmen. "Anyway, look, the point is I've brought you your homework." He ducked out into the hall and returned with a small suitcase. "Bingo!" The locks snapped open and Johanna found herself gazing on a sea of colour. Yarns in unimaginable shades, some already wound on cops, some in hanks, had been packed into the case. Enchantment robbed her of breath. Shay misinterpreted this. "Relax, love, joke! I really brought them back for the shop. Harry wants to put them on display in the window. With some other odds and bobs I've also got out in the car if you're interested."

"Such as?"

"Well, come and see. A warping board, for one thing, and a loom."

"A *loom*? In the car?"

"Oh, just a table one. Sort of a curiosity now. They all have foot looms with fly shuttles. I don't know how much you'd get done on this." He showed it to her, grinning. "But it will serve Harry's needs."

It would also miraculously serve hers. "How long before he has to get it?"

"Oh, I don't know. Monday, Tuesday, Wednesday. Why?" Shay was staring at her.

"Then—will you bring it into the house, please, Shay,

and let me have it? Just for a few days. And don't tell anyone. Specially not your father. It might be a terrible flop, you see, but I do know how to weave. It was part of my course. I'm not a designer. I . . ." She hadn't meant to lie, it had just slipped out.

"Well, I hardly expected you were," Shay smiled. "That would be a bit too much even for St. Anthony! Still, have a go by all means, see what pops up." He laughed. "Myles used to say that. Oh, you'd have fallen for *him*, Jo," he concluded. "And he'd have been good for you. He'd soon have made you forget that chap you're fretting for. I'd lay my shirt on it."

"Shay." It was only about three weeks since she'd first met him, since, standing at another car, white instead of yellow, something about him had touched the heart that had seemed so dead.

"Yes, pet?" His hand came chummily down on her shoulder.

"Nothing," she said smilingly.

She had been wrong, precipitous, disloyal. Quite hateful. It was just that hearing him say it like that, about Myles, as though she'd never love anyone else, she had thought, at first gropingly, then with more certainty: "I don't think that's true. I don't think I am fretting—now."

Later that evening, Johanna, kneeling on her sage green carpet, was thinking about the sky, the sky in summer over Black Glen. She took up the cobalt hank, laid it beside a white one, and tossed it away. Too sharp, too bright. It had alum in it. Turquoise gave a better result. But in Ireland you seldom got a day when there wasn't a bit of cloud about, like a beard or a tongue or the Never-Never-Land. Purple? She laid it in place and frowned. Too strong a contrast. What, then? And she tried a royal blue. Now something to suggest evening when the blue faded out to pale green and the pink crept in. Light green and pink . . .

"What are we going to do with you?" the voice asked. Douglas O'Malley was standing on the threshold. "I did knock several times. I was wondering if I'd been the fire engine would you even have noticed?"

76

"Sorry." She would have scrambled up, but astonishingly he had lowered himself to the floor. "Long way down for old bones," he remarked cheerfully. "Let's see. What are you doing?"

It was the last thing she wanted, but there seemed no avoiding it. Amazingly, he seemed to know what he was looking at. He turned over the colours, lifted the pink, tried another shade and, with a smile, put back the one she'd chosen. "Right first time," he allowed.

It was time to offer an explanation. "Shay brought these back from the factory. I'm just . . . well . . ."

"I know. You told me. You're studying tweed." The face was utterly impassive.

"Yes," she agreed lamely, "sort of. I . . . is that the time?" She had seen it suddenly, just ten o'clock. "Heavens, it can't be! I had no idea. I thought it was about half past eight. I'll . . ."

"I hope you will some time," he said smoothly, taking up a hank of yellow and depositing it on another part of the carpet. "Let me say what I came for." Another yellow, more of a limey tone, went against the first one. She watched fascinated. There was something so easy about it and something very sure.

"If I may make a poor return for the dinner you were kind enough to offer me, there's coffee on the go upstairs."

"Oh!" Talk about the mountain coming to Mohamet, she wondered if it had ever sat on his bedroom carpet. "Thanks, I'd love some." She looked at the downbent head and the hand now hovering over a green cop. "May I just comb my hair?"

"You may do anything you like, within reason," the voice pronounced as the hand dug triumphantly into the pile for an olive shade. "And while you're doing it and I'm making my cornfield there are a few things I want to say to you."

"Well." Looking in the mirror,. she could see that he was now sitting up, hugging his knees and addressing her back. "First of all I'm sorry to say my mother's had a setback, not serious, I hope, but it means she won't be home next week as I'd thought. And that, in turn, means I won't be able to let you go for a while longer."

*Let her go?* The comb stayed and Johanna's eyes widened.

"I'd felt that if my mother got home in the middle of next week and you stayed to tide her over for another ten days, we could let you go back to your studies tomorrow fortnight. Three weeks was the kind of time I'd had in mind for this job. It looks now as if it could be nearer six. Will that be all right?"

"Oh—*yes.*" She was ashamed of the fact that relief and pleasure came first, concern for Sheila O'Malley second.

"Thanks," he said when she had expressed this. "I'm afraid the reason for the setback isn't a hundred miles away and since you may find a rather troubled atmosphere when we go up I thought I'd better warn you. You probably know about Young O'Malley?" Johanna nodded. "For obvious reasons my mother wanted it strangled at birth, my father has just revived it and given it to Shay with his blessing. Geraldine, who as I've told you guards my mother like a dragon, is quite steamed up about it. Shay, as you have probably seen, thinks my father can do no wrong." He managed to sound completely detached. "The pair of them will probably be at each other's throats by the time we get there."

"What do *you* think, Mr. O'Malley?" Johanna risked.

"Douglas," he said casually. "If you can manage to remember. And what do I think about what?"

"Young O'Malley?"

"How funny." He looked at her, his head on one side. "That's the first time that question has ever been asked."

First, second, third or fourth, it didn't seem that he was going to answer it.

"We want the neutral, don't we? White, I think." He dropped the last hank beside the waiting five. Dumbly, Johanna watched. This was the son who'd branched off, who cared nothing for tweed. But no one who didn't care could have handled the yarns like that or placed the colours so unerringly.

"I didn't know you went in for this sort of thing." She gestured towards the coloured hanks.

He answered her seriously. "I don't know that I do. I think it's more that a lot of this sort of thing went into me when I was in the making. I had a wonderful old grandfather, I remember him quite well."

"So had Shay! He told me about him."

"Yes. Brendan O'Connor. He put the rest into me. I sat on his doorstep all day and every day when I was a kid, not so much for the weaving I'll admit as the stories. They don't grow them like Brendan any more, more's the pity. Time was when every village in Ireland had its storyteller. He was Carrickdoo's. However," he checked, "it's time we went aloft."

Douglas's sitting-room looked charming by the light of its golden lamps, but as he had prophesied, its atmosphere was not as tranquil. Geraldine was sitting on the edge of a dark blue armchair, Shay was standing by the window and both looked very tense.

"Sorry to keep you. We were making a cornfield," Douglas announced provocatively.

The gambit was ignored. "I've been telling Shay the position about your mother and how worried you are," Geraldine began.

"Oh yes?" Douglas glanced affably from one to the other. "Well, one bother is solved anyway. Jo's available to stay as long as we need her."

It might have taken a load off his mind, but for some reason it seemed to have the opposite effect on Geraldine's. "I thought you had to go back in three weeks," she said quickly.

"Well—no, actually not till September," Johanna murmured.

"So!" Douglas said cheerily. "That's one thing less for you to worry about, my dear."

"I'm afraid it's a very small thing," Johanna put in modestly. "But I will do my best."

"I'm sure you will," Geraldine said drily. Tonight she looked much younger, indeed hardly older than Shay and as typically Irish. Her long dark hair which before had been swirled up and coiled now hung in a blue-black cloud to her shoulders.

The coffee was excellent, but it was not the most convivial of evenings. Johanna had never seen Shay so quiet. It was Douglas who made the running, once jokingly taking a fold of Geraldine's skirt in his hand and saying: "Here, Jo, something else for that *magnum opus* of *yours*. Crios cloth. Woven in the Aran Islands. The fishermen used to wear belts of it for good luck."

It was the curiously woven dress Geraldine had been wearing that first day in O'Malley House, its stripes matchstick thin and beautifully coloured. Johanna examined it eagerly and Douglas went on to tell her that the intricate patterns in which the traditional Aran sweaters were knitted had also served a purpose for the fisher folk, this time a tragic one. A body washed up at sea could often be identified by them.

"And on the subject of weaving," he continued, "I was going to suggest that you do it here. There's more room and you'd have a lot more peace. I'm practically always out, so I wouldn't get in your hair."

"I mean it," he added as she hesitated. "The phone's there if my father wants you and I can give you a spare key."

She was sorely tempted. Once she got to the stage of weaving her pattern there was no place downstairs where she could set up the loom away from Alice's scrutiny. "It's very good of you."

"I know. Saint Anthony couldn't have returned you to a better person," he assured her.

The coffee pot drained and the last sandwich accounted for, Geraldine brushed aside Johanna's offer to help with the chores. "Heavens, no, you get enough of it. This is my job." The smile was warm and friendly. Under its impact Johanna, making her excuses to Douglas, began to feel that after all Geraldine Baldwin did not dislike her.

"Pleasure. Any time. And don't forget what I said about the weaving," Douglas said, smiling from the top of the staircase.

Shay who had gone down first stood aside as Johanna's feet gained the terrace. She smiled, assuming he was going to accompany her to the kitchen door, but to her astonishment he pushed past her and bolted back up the steps he had just descended. "I've the car still out, Doug. I could run Gerry home."

"Hold on, I'll ask her," Douglas's voice replied. There was a second's pause and then it sounded again.

"It's all right, thanks, I'll take her. She wants to finish up here."

If Shay answered it was inaudible and to Johanna, watching, he hardly seemed to look at the stairs as he hurtled down them. Something as shocking, when she saw it in the bright white glare of the kitchen, was his face.

"Is something wrong?" she asked timidly.

"No," he snapped, making for the door into the hall.

"Aren't you going to put away your car?"

Shay halted, looked about him desperately, retorted: "Hang the car!" and was gone.

So, to crown things, was Smokey the cat when she went to call him. It was after eleven; she called, softly so as not to wake Matthew, and searched under every bush in the garden, but there was no sign of the trotting grey form. She didn't think Smokey cared for her, he always ran from her advances, excepting only when he felt in the mood to eat. And tonight Shay had run from her too. Something was wrong there, so terribly wrong that he could not share it. She knew the feeling, she had cause to. When you had loved tragically there was no ear on earth to which you could, at first anyway, lay bare your grief. And Shay had loved like that. He'd told her that much. Nothing more.

"Smokey! Smokey! Smokey!" she called, stumbling wearily round the swimming pool.

Perhaps it was her eyes searching for the cat's shape that made other impressions suddenly clear . . . Shay's taut figure and the flags of coral in Geraldine's cheeks . . . Shay's obsessive charge up the staircase . . . Shay last Saturday saying "They'll make a go of it one of these fine days" and then sitting there, not moving, even when the lights turned green . . . *Shay and Geraldine* . . .

She didn't know why it should have been such a shock, but shock it was, and it seemed to drain her last vestige of energy. She stood between the rosebeds irresolute and exhausted.

"What's the trouble? Don't say you're locked out?" Geraldine, now with a cardigan slung across her shoulders, approached her in the gloom. "I noticed you from over there." She pointed in the direction of the garage belonging to Douglas. "What's wrong?"

81

The kind tone brought down Johanna's defences. "It's Smokey," she said despairingly. "I just can't find him. I've been looking for ages."

"Oh, heavens," Geraldine said with warming exasperation. "Does he do this often?"

"Every night, but this is the worst ever." Johanna gave another soft call. "And I don't want to wake Mr. O'Malley, particularly when he hasn't been well."

"Well, up to you, of course." Geraldine glanced over her shoulder. "Sorry, there's Doug. I'll have to go. You worry too much!" she called chummily as she ran.

There had been a lot of worry in the day, Johanna thought, and at that moment, alone and very tired, it made most depressing thinking. However, perhaps she did. A last unavailing look for Smokey and she went in to bed.

It was hard to get to sleep; so many things, happy and unhappy, coursed through her mind—Smokey, Shay, Sheila O'Malley, Matthew's indisposition, and Douglas, first cutting her down to size and then being so kind. Of all the day's moments those "making the cornfield" lingered the most persistently. She dropped off at last and woke with a start, it seemed only five minutes later. But it wasn't. The room was bright and someone was hammering on the door.

"Are you decent?" Shay's voice called.

She rubbed her eyes and said: "Yes."

"I was afraid of that," he retorted, and opened the door. Surprise number one was the cup of tea in his hand, surprise number two the fact that although it was Saturday he was immaculate in a dark business suit.

"Just off, alas." He glanced at his wrist. "The boss had this all lined up. It's—er—" his colour rose slightly— "Young O'Malley. The boy's going to have his picture took."

"You mean—*you're* going to be the prototype!"

"Get an earful of that now! Where does she get it from?" he mocked. "Yes, love, couldn't have put it better myself. We've finally grasped the nettle."

It was the perfect solution, the scheme preserved and Sheila O'Malley spared the anguish of seeing Myles's postered face. Everything fitted, age, appearance, even name. Enthusiastically, Johanna said so.

"Hope so," Shay answered seriously. "Well, I'd better be off." He moved to the door, halted and came back. "Look, love, about last night. I made an unfunny ass of myself. Sorry."

"Oh, Shay, don't apologize," Johanna begged. "I just wish I could help, that's all."

"You have," he said abruptly. "And you do. You're here and you're sweet, and that means a lot, I can tell you. I've had the message from Gerry several times, you know, loud and clear. Most days it's okay, it doesn't hurt, just sometimes I still come apart. Anyway, next time it happens you run for cover."

She called after him, remembering last night's truant: "Did you see Smokey around?" and got the answer she'd anticipated: "No, thank heaven."

Ten minutes later she searched herself, searched everywhere, windowsills, driveway, garden and under every bush. There was no sign at all. And then she went right down to the gate and looked up and down the road. Looking left, the way Shay would have driven, it was all quite clear. Looking right, to the roadhouse, a pale grey bundle lay stretched at the side of the road.

In the first dazed second it meant nothing, but soon her brain abandoned its futile defence. It was Smokey. Her legs hardly holding her, she turned and walked back up the drive.

Except Matthew, there was no one to face. She tried Douglas's bell, but got no answer, and his car was gone from the garage. Alice had asked leave to see a wedding on her way in and was not due for an hour. She told Matthew when she took away his tray. "All right, can't be helped," he said curtly, sounding more annoyed than upset. "Just bring him in."

Douglas would have to do that. She couldn't, not for diamonds; she couldn't even look. "Shut your eyes, darling, don't look," her mother had always said in the dim past when there had been these little tragedies on or about Dykes Lynn. It died hard.

Some time later, and a very long time it seemed, Douglas's car came back up the drive and she ran out to meet him, gulping the story in eight agonized words:

"Mr. O'Malley (it was no occasion for 'Douglas'), it's Smokey! He's been run over."

She'd been bottling it up, framing phrases, picturing the effect on Sheila O'Malley, wondering if the old cat had been hurt or if there had been a moment of panic before the impact. Now with the last word her mouth turned to water, salty, cold.

An arm went round her, a hand, big and comforting, gripped her shoulder. "Now then, take it easy."

She sat weakly in the little surgery and the scene cleared . . . olive green shirt with buttoned collar, mustard knitted tie, above them calm dark grey eyes. "How did it happen?"

"I don't know."

The grey eyes changed as again she stumbled miserably through the story. "Well, all right. It's unfortunate, but it can't be helped. The cat's troubles at least are over."

She said: "Yes," wretchedly, not liking what he had not said. She'd been irresponsible and he would now have the job of telling his mother.

"What have you done with him?"

She started. "I—nothing. I just saw him. On the road." She jerked her head in the direction of the sad discovery.

"He *was killed?*"

"I—he must be—he's not moving."

"Good gr—!" he checked sharply and got to his feet. "All right. I'll get him."

The surgery door opened and shut and the stocky tweed-jacketed figure went striding down the drive to return a few minutes later with Smokey's still form in his arms.

"We can take that one as read. Quite instantaneous, I'd say. I was just afraid . . ." he did not finish. There was no need to. Johanna had got the message. It was an hour since she'd first seen the cat by the roadside. For all she knew—and Douglas could hardly be blamed if he had thought for all she cared—it could have been lying there all that time alive and in agony.

"If you're squeamish about this sort of thing better clear off," Douglas said reasonably. "I'm going to bury him before Alice comes in."

84

"Can I help?" Johanna faltered, trying not to look and trying at the same time not to look away.

This Douglas did not miss. "Safer not, I think. I don't want you fainting on my hands." He went off across the lawn with his burden.

Going down the garden before lunch to replenish the flower vases, Johanna found the freshly turned earth where she had seen Douglas digging and as she was looking at it he came along.

"Thanks for the coffee. Alice said you had sent it. Most welcome." He smiled. "And this afternoon have yourself an outing, as our American cousins would say. Get Shay to drive you somewhere."

When she did not answer he peered at her face. "And don't worry about that." He glanced at the turned earth. "It was probably a blessing in disguise. I'd have put him down months ago if he'd been mine. Nor my mother either," he appended abruptly. "I've no doubt Alice has been keening about her all morning, but it's far less than her due. She is, I can assure you, plenty tough."

That very thought had been in the back of Johanna's own mind.

"Come on." The arm went round her shoulder. "This is no place to be standing round in. I'm not sentimental over animals' graves, don't think it. I just like to do right by them when their time comes."


CHAPTER EIGHT

IT SEEMED that Johanna had now had her baptism of fire, for after the first week everything settled down.

Matthew on new tablets had three or four practically pain-free days, in consequence of which he had Shay drive him into the office. "You should have seen him!" Shay reported that evening. "He went through the place like a bomb. At least like a bomb on sticks!" Translated, this meant that a whole new department had been set up to deal with Young O'Malley and most of the copy submitted by the advertising consultants had been thrown out.

A general trail of chaos had been left behind, but Matthew returned to Knockbeg looking as Johanna felt he must have looked before his illness, clear-eyed, quick-smiled, punctuating every sentence with a gesture.

"The golden rule, Johanna, is never to accept anything the first time because it can always be done better," he informed her at dinner. "The one exception, of course, is your cooking!"

Seeing him in this mood of liberation, gay, enthusiastic, almost boy-like, Johanna wondered yet again what had gone wrong between him and Sheila. Except for that one angry outburst over Young O'Malley Matthew had never once mentioned his wife.

Shay was in Dublin all that week and spent a large part of it showing Johanna the town. The promised meal at the roadhouse was followed by supper in a rooftop restaurant, dinner at the airport and a play and punch at the country mansion headquarters of the Georgian Society. The days rocketing by could have been trade-marked "Young O'Malley". They were so hedonistic. Not even Myles had given her such a good time.

"Don't you think we should stay in tonight?" she asked doubtfully once. "After all, I am the housekeeper and we've been out every night this week."

Shay brushed aside all scruples. "Exactly, love; house-keeper, not nurse. And anyway, Matt's up to his eyeballs and happy as Larry. It's only when he's not well enough to do it himself that he needs people and then believe me he'll soon let us know." He added another shrewd comment that he might wake up in the morning and find himself "belting off" to Donegal for a further spell, so it behoved them to make hay while the sun shone.

In the mad merry whirl she had hardly exchanged two words with Douglas all week.

By a coincidence that evening she bumped into him outside the surgery. "Douglas," she said awkwardly, "I wanted to ask you. Is it all right Shay and I going out so much? Your father's been alone almost every night."

"No, he hasn't," Douglas replied promptly. "Geraldine and I have usually looked in. Anyway, he's so well at the moment he doesn't need nursing." Exactly what Shay had said. "So it's perfectly all right," he concluded kindly. "Only too glad to see you enjoying yourselves. Shay needs a break. To be vulgar, he practically works his guts out for us. I'm delighted to see him having the chance to relax."

"I'm afraid I haven't been getting on very fast with the—er—cornfield."

"Oh, that!" he laughed. "You weren't meant to take that seriously, you know. Forget it."

For no logical reason the words echoed coldly.

"What doing?" Shay asked a short time later when she summoned up the courage to tell him that she had a plan for after dinner. "Oh, the weaving. Do you really want to?"

She did. That morning she had wound the last lengths of yarn round the pegs on the warping board. Now it had to be disengaged and beamed on to the loom and "beaming on"' could not be done without help. Shay, as ever good-natured, agreed to assist and after dinner he carried all the paraphernalia up to the dormer flat.

"Be my guest," Douglas said amicably, opening the door. "Put it wherever you like, it won't be in my way. I'll probably be back before you finish. If not, help yourselves. You know where everything is." He went off, Flann at his heels, to take evening surgery.

"They say this is like life, don't they?" Shay observed as he turned the cog wheel, Johanna letting the chained warp in her hands go little by little. "Mind, love, don't let it slip. Keep a good steady pull. That's it! Right. Now we'll thread up." Shay's deft fingers took a length of hemp and tied the cross sticks. It couldn't be hurried because the pattern depended on how the warp was threaded through the heddle loops and Shay worked easily and placidly. Watching, she thought she was seeing his other side, the side that was rooted in the hills of Donegal where he had been taught his grandfather's skills.

Everything was set up and she'd thrown her first shuttles across the shed when Douglas returned. Geraldine was with him. She'd been giving him a hand in place of his usual student helper who was on holiday.

"Anyone for tennis?" Douglas asked seriously.

"Yes, please, long and cool," Shay answered as Johanna stared.

"It's a joke," Geraldine explained kindly. "You know —coffee—beer—what have you?" Johanna would never have guessed and she felt obtuse. She disappeared into the kitchen to make coffee. When she returned Geraldine and Shay were sitting side by side on the sofa.

"Jo love, I've got bad news for you." Shay was regarding her unhappily.

"What?" She felt her eyes widen as they always did when she was afraid.

Shay must have seen this. He sighed. "Oh, Gerry, surely to God . . ."

"Shay, I am *sorry*, terribly sorry. I can't do anything," Geraldine said.

"Well, it's the loom," Shay said desperately. "It's got to go back in the morning."

"Back . . ." Now Johanna was remembering. It was wanted in O'Malley House for a window display. "Oh no!" The words came out involuntarily. "I only want it a few more days."

"We should have had it last Monday," Geraldine pointed out gently.

"What for?" Douglas asked suddenly.

It was explained. The window dressers were due in the morning. "We've had quite a week of it," Geraldine mentioned reasonably. "When Mr. O'Malley left on Wednesday nobody knew which end was up. Those two he took for Young O'Malley, there's just nobody to do the work he took them off. Jim Corrigan's just about round the bend. He was on the verge of giving notice only I calmed him down."

"Was he now?" Douglas asked expressionlessly. Jim Corrigan, Johanna recalled, was office manager.

"It is a bit rough," Shay murmured. "I mean, I know the boss is a ruddy marvel, but he does leave a trail behind him."

"Has *he* asked for the loom to be returned?" Douglas questioned once more.

"No," said Shay, and looked helplessly at Geraldine.

It was more subtle than that, she explained. Last Monday she'd put the window dresser off and perhaps it wouldn't have mattered making another postponement if in the meantime there had not been Matthew's chaos and Jim's ultimatum that if anyone else countermanded his instructions he'd pack it in. "I can't ask him to change again. Like as not he'd fly straight up to Mrs. O'Malley and worry her with it."

"If he did fly up he wouldn't be let see her," Douglas said shortly.

"Well, I've the greatest sympathy with Jim." Geraldine's cards came down flat on the table. "Honestly, Doug, he's between the devil and the deep blue sea. I sometimes wonder how he sticks it."

There was silence. Then: "Yes," Douglas pronounced slowly. "*I* wonder that continually."

"So there it is." Geraldine concluded. "And I am sorry. But there's not a thing I can do."

The disappointment was agonizing, but Johanna could see the justice of the argument. And there *had* been all those nights when she'd gone out. Nights she'd enjoyed, she reminded herself. No use saying Shay had taken her against her will. She'd had her cake, she couldn't expect it at the other end as well.

"No, of course not," she said. "It probably wouldn't have been any good anyway."

A hand touched her arm. "Would you like to give me a hand outside?" Douglas asked quietly.

"Times like these I prefer to make myself scarce," he explained, carrying the cups to the sink. "Sorry about the loom." He handed her a tea towel. "Would Wednesday have done?"

She nodded, adding hastily that it didn't matter.

"No. That's what I felt. It's best not to interfere," Douglas agreed. "As you may have noticed, I never do." She had noticed it, so it was unnecessary to underline the fact that she need expect no help from him.

"By the way, I wanted to ask you," he was saying. "What have you done to Alice? Butter wouldn't melt in her mouth these days. The old place," he added severely, "doesn't seem the same somehow."

Johanna stared suspiciously at the solemn eyes. It was true that Alice all week had stayed docile and obliging. It had in fact seemed like a miracle. But had she once again done wrong?

"I'm sorry—" she began.

"Oh, not again!" he implored. "If I were to lay down a penny for every time you've said I'm sorry lately, dear

knows where they'd end up. Great Yarmouth perhaps!"
His look was strangely gentle. "Still homesick?"

*Still*—he must have been thinking of that first night
out on the hill when she'd wanted desperately to run away.

"No," she replied truthfully, and reverted, "Does it
matter?"

"What?"

"Alice changing?"

"Let's just say I wish you could change a few more of
us like that," he said. "And let's just say also that you
have the makings."

"Of—what?" she breathed. It was a strange, breath-
less moment. His face seemed to have come so near her
own, and it looked—different. Shyly she jerked hers away.

"A *bean a tighe*," he said. "For the benefit of foreigners
—the woman of the house."

"Oh! You mean—housekeeper?" she asked uncertainly.

There was another odd little pause.

"Yes, housekeeper. What else?" he said, but flatly,
she thought. And then: "*Does* it matter?"

She was hanging up the tea towel and she started. It
did matter. Suddenly it mattered above everything else
that she should have "the makings". It had mattered
first because of Myles and the needs of the household.
Now it mattered because . . .

"Does what matter?" she questioned abruptly.

"The loom." His expression was now again in the care
of those "keeping" grey eyes.

"Oh . . ." What did you think he meant? she asked
herself. *What did you think he meant?* "Yes," she answered
truthfully, "it does, but I understand. And I wouldn't
want there to be trouble."

"There won't be," he said placidly.

Next morning when Douglas emerged from Matthew's
room, he put his head into the kitchen where Alice was
washing up, Johanna making pastry and Shay cleaning
his shoes.

"Oh, by the way, that's all right about the loom. Keep
it till Wednesday. I had a word with Jim." The head
withdrew before either Johanna or Shay could find breath.

"He said he never interfered." Johanna recovered first.

90

"And believe me, he never has before." Shay seemed to have been smitten by an attack of paralysis. He stood goggling, the shoebrush in his hand. "The original non-aggressionist, makes a fetish of it." He looked at her. "Well, I don't know, young Jo. What did you do to him in the wood last night?"

It was a happy morning. Alice, still in her co-operative cycle, agreed to watch the lunch and Johanna prepared it and dashed away to the flat. She was hard at work when the door bell rang.

On the balcony, a girl, tall, slim, dark-haired and probably in her late twenties, said apologetically: "I suppose this is quite the wrong moment to catch Mr. O'Malley?"

Johanna confirmed that Douglas was out and the caller sighed. "Oh dear, I wanted to explain because I know he'll be fed up with us." For the first time Johanna noticed the zip-fastened shopping bag on the floor. Intuition told her precisely what would follow.

"I'm Jane Lamb. My nephew, Mark, got this kitten two weeks ago. I'm afraid I can't keep it at present." She explained that her husband's job was taking him for six weeks to Central Africa and that, while she had expected to be staying at home, there had now been a pressing invitation to go to her in-laws in Scotland for the summer. "They simply won't take no," she finished.

"Perhaps Mr. O'Malley will board it till September . . ." Jane Lamb hesitated.

Johanna thought she had better get this clear. "Then you do want it back, Mrs. Lamb?"

There was a pause. "I will take it back, certainly," Jane Lamb said firmly. There seemed to be a difference. Johanna waited. "The truth is, it's a little villain. I haven't a nylon to my name. Its name's Clootie, by the way."

Johanna accepted custody, there seemed to be no alternative.

Douglas kept quiet about his lunch and dinner arrangements. He was not the sort to starve, but he certainly couldn't have time to prepare anything really tasty. To-day, for instance, he had said he would not be back until twelve-thirty, and afternoon surgery began at two. An unauthorized peep into his cupboards confirmed that they were disconcertingly bare, while downstairs under Alice's eye quite a pleasant meal was cooking, beefburgers to be served with a mixed salad and apples being baked in cider sauce.

Anyway Clootie, at this moment rampant on the draining board, his long white belly arched as he dabbed at the dish mop, had to be considered.

She poked round, hoping to find some of the pretty plates and fireproof dishes that the family kitchen had in such abundance, but all Douglas's stock were plain white, and from the state of his tablecloths, laundered but creased from months of disuse, it looked as though he ate off the bare boards. She found a gay one at last, emerald green linen, still packed in a cellophane lidded box.

How like a man not to use it, never to bother about himself. Firmly she took it out and spread it, finding a striped weave napkin and a pretty rush mat to go with it.

Even the plain white plate didn't look too bad with the food on it, cucumber discs, curls of lettuce, tomato and two fat brown beefburgers, her own, as a matter of fact, but he need not know. Suddenly she was singing, dancing about the kitchen, flicking Clootie's head, dressing the salad with lemon juice, sprinkling it with parsley. The baked apple she'd had to borrow a dish for, pale green so that against it the golden-fleshed fruit in its golden sauce and stuck over with toasted almonds looked quite luxurious.

At something before one, the big green estate car came up the drive and Douglas got out and opened the back door for Flann. He looked up mechanically at the balcony, saw her and waved. The darkish hair frisked on his forehead and his eyes were narrowed against the sun. She didn't know quite what came over her as she ran down the staircase to meet him.

"Hullo," he said, in just that uneffusive way that some weeks ago had been so off-putting.

"You've got a visitor," she said.

"At this hour! Who is it?"

"I didn't quite catch the name," she said brazenly, and grabbed the hand nearest her. It was quite easy really. The hand, warm and large, stayed quite naturally in hers and he looked neither astonished nor angry. She started thinking that this was what life was all about, having a meal on the table, hearing a car stop in the drive, seeing a man wave at you, feeling a hand in yours—and then, like a thunderclap, as they reached the top of the staircase, she remembered Geraldine. "One of these fine days" would become a commonplace for Douglas, no more white plates, no more creased tablecloths . . .

Why ever had she thought that he needed warmth and welcoming? He could not possibly be lonely, he had a girl of his own. On the instant her hand slipped out of his.

"Now, see what you get for uncrossing your fingers!"

In the middle of the emerald green cloth was Clootie licking the butter.

"Oh, *stone the crows!*" Douglas groaned disgustedly.

A few minutes later he said something else. "What is all this?"

"Lunch. What does it look like?" Johanna replied briskly. "I was getting it for Clootie. I thought you might as well share it."

"Oh, did you?" Sad to say he did not look anything like enraptured. "Well, look, I know you meant well, but as I've told you before, I can look after myself."

"Oh, you can, can you?" Johanna had reached both the door and the end of her tether. "Bully for you!" she yelled. "And just as well. I'm certainly not going to do anything else for that matter, not ever, not if you ask on bended knee. And that's flat!" She let the door go. It banged and she flew heedlessly down the stairs.

Already she was ashamed of her outburst and what had given rise to it. She should have realized that you could not take liberties with a man like Douglas. Matthew's abrupt "Sampled our pool yet?" made up her mind for her.

The pool certainly had the loveliest of settings—satin-striped lawn, rose beds and the sentinel amethyst hills. After the swim she took off her cap, shook out her hair and stretched on the sunbaked paving. Before long her eyes had closed.

Some time later she opened them slowly, flexed her ankles and sat up. In the slow, delicious way that follows sleep the world impinged again—particles spinning in the long rays of sunshine, silver dazzles on the turquoise water, dust on the honey-coloured stone and—sleepy no longer, her eyes flew open—a figure sitting on the edge of the pool, trouser legs hitched up, feet dangling in the water.

Blinking, she studied him, broad hunched shoulders, white shirt, suntanned legs and deep-hewn eyes now turned in her direction.

"Hullo," he said.

"Hullo. I—I—didn't see you," Johanna responded brilliantly.

"No?" he queried. "You had your eyes shut."

She watched fascinated as one large foot splashed gently. But she was not going to speak. *Definitely* she was not going to speak.

"That was a nice lunch," he observed and, when she still did not speak, looked round at her. "And I was rude," he said simply. "So what are you going to do with me?"

For a scaring moment, Johanna was afraid she was going to cry. She was afraid of other things too, but she shoved them away again.

"I must go," he said, and sat there. He couldn't go till his feet dried and he could put on his shoes.

"So must I." She looked as if she meant it, and why was she looking at him like that? The sepia eyes were fixed on him, the rose-pink mouth about to open. *She needn't be afraid, I wouldn't touch her, doesn't she know that?* It riled that obviously she didn't, the more so because he had seen her with Shay, once even towelling his hair.

Dammit, why couldn't he have kept his feelings about the lunch to himself? It was just that not an hour before, when he'd dropped in on Geraldine to make arrangements about a dinner party that night, and had mentioned that he'd solved the problem of the loom, she had said laughingly: "I'm so glad, she's a nice kid, and it's rather sweet really the way she thinks of you." "Thinks of me?" he had echoed, and Geraldine had checked and said: "Oh lor'! It was strictly girl talk, I'm afraid, so don't let on I've told you. She thinks the reason you're so different from Shay is that you're too much alone and have got into a rut." "Oh, she does, does she?" he'd chuckled. "I suppose, next, she'll be calling me an old fuddy-duddy!" And Geraldine's face had changed to a half smile and suddenly embarrassed eyes. "Oh no, Doug," she'd said uncertainly, "I'm sure—she never would." So he'd not been left in the smallest doubt that Johanna had already used the term.

And quite naturally, he'd reasoned as he'd driven home, he was thirteen years her senior and no girl except Geraldine had ever looked twice at him when Myles and Shay were around. And unless they were kids or the owners of patients, he never knew what to say to them anyway.

And then as he'd got out of the car, down the steps she had come like a rocket, brown fringe grazing the top of her eyebrows, and in that short bright blue thing with the straps, and for a moment . . . but he'd been mad. Inside, there had been all the proof anyone needed that he was being "rescued", and that a warm twenty-year-old heart was looking upon him with compassion.

Well, he didn't think the compassion would last much longer. In fact, it had already given place to this uncertain timidity. Plainly she was thinking that the kind old fuddy-duddy was preferable to the boor who had received her good deed so harshly.

"Now I really must go," he slipped his feet into his shoes. "I've still a call to make before I pick Geraldine up." He went striding across the lawn.

The sun had shifted also and some grey had stolen into the turquoise of the pool. The mountains too were darker as Johanna stared at them.

It's time you grew up, Jo Dykes, she said, and went slowly into the house.

# CHAPTER NINE

THE next day Flann became a father. "Not his first time, hers," Douglas said when the telephone call came. "And her owner's," he added ambiguously, and was off. The bitch had nine (one dead) and trouble, so they did not see Douglas for the rest of the afternoon. Johanna relayed the information to Geraldine when she arrived.

"Well, I wonder if you . . ." Geraldine checked. "No, I don't suppose you could." She came and looked the loom over with quite a friendly smile. "You know that is really very pretty."

"Thank you." On the principle of one kind word deserving another, Johanna asked what the other had been going to say.

"Oh, just something I was looking for and thought you might have seen around. An advertisement, actually." Idly Geraldine lifted a cushion. "We had it last night. Brought it back from the friends we dined with. Those new houses they're putting up in Sandyford."

New houses! Johanna wondered why the room should suddenly seem so quiet. She hadn't seen the advertisement, but she got up and joined in the search.

"Doesn't matter," Geraldine said after some minutes. "He's probably got it on him. We're going down to take a look at them when he comes back." She broke off to observe that something seemed to be happening in the kitchen. Something was. Shay had gone in to get a drink of water. He came out looking green with Clootie hanging on to one leg of his trousers. Johanna had already discovered that Jane Lamb's lament about nylons had been no exaggeration. It was not always easy to like Clootie, nor Douglas either when he remarked as he had done that morning: "Well, why did you take him back?"

Monday and Tuesday were edgy days. Alice made bones about being asked to watch the lunch again. Clootie, having a violent game with the telephone cord, succeeded in putting the kitchen instrument out of action, and Matthew, not pleased in the first place, became almost violent himself at the delay in getting it repaired. Douglas, hearing the story, said that he supposed in the long run he would have to put the kitten down.

"Johanna, have I done something to upset you?" Douglas asked on Tuesday night.

She started, flushing. "Of course not."

"That's all right, then. I just thought that you seemed very quiet."

"I was wondering," she said jerkily. "If there's any more news of your mother coming home."

He looked at her. "Yes, as a matter of fact, I was going to tell you. It won't be long now. Are you thinking about your own plans?"

"Yes." She strove to appear composed. "But there's no hurry, of course. I shall stay as long as you need me. That was the bargain."

"Yes. Well—thanks," Douglas said a trifle lamely. "I'll let you know as soon as I can." A thought seemed to strike him and he paused. "Oh, by the way, they'll want the loom back tomorrow, won't they?"

"Yes. Shay's looking after it. I've finished." She had not meant to sound curt, just adult. Unfortunately, like almost every other encounter they'd had since Saturday this one, too, was going wrong.

"Well, aren't you going to show me the masterpieces?" he came back expectantly. He did not always look wall-like, sometimes he had rather an anxious air. This was one of the times.

Johanna had been hoping foolishly that he would forget about the weaving. It had proved far more difficult than she'd expected and the pieces were amateurish in the extreme.

"You won't think much of them," she said desperately.

"Let me be the judge of that," he returned.

Reluctantly, she fetched them, the one a blending of blues and white with a twill of carmine pink and a knop of almond green, the other in similar pattern, a mixture of the gold and limey shades with an orange knop.

"I'm afraid I'm not a weaver," she said.

"I can see that." She felt the large thumb need not have gone to the place where she was conscious of having "milked" the threads in beaming. "However, I don't think that was the purpose of the exercise. Surely we wanted to find out if you could come up with the answer to Felgate-Winter and/or Young O'Malley."

Ego went up a bit. She was pleased with the colours and the pattern was well broken. "Well?" she ventured at last.

"Are you sure you want to know?" Douglas enquired meaningly. There was a most unattractive gleam in his eye.

"Of course," she said shortly.

The gleam had now become a glisten. "In one word—fuddy-duddy!" You would think he enjoyed saying it.

It was unfair, the colours were fresh and attractive,

she'd willingly wear either blending and it was pretty cool —she'd like to see him turn out anything as nice. Fuddy-duddy indeed! How dare he?

"I thought they were quite pretty," she bristled.

"They are," he agreed. "They're pretty and charming, and O'Malleys have been making tweeds like them for the past fifty years. And if you think they're suitable for Young O'Malley then I suggest you keep them out of my father's way, that's all!"

She made a last try for the yellow. "I think this is exactly like a cornfield."

"My dear Jo, that's the trouble, it shouldn't. Not these days. No one should ever be able to know for sure."

"Must you be so cynical?"

"I'm not." Gleam and glisten had disappeared. "Nowadays people want to be excited and puzzled. Everything has to be just that little bit different. Even I know that. Judging by these," he lifted the samples of tweed, "you don't." He turned up his lip at them and laid them down. "Fuddy-duddy!" he said again.

In the midst of it all the thing that rankled most was the almost gloating tone of the last "Fuddy-duddy!" He had *wanted* to say it, he had *enjoyed* saying it. Why?

She was glad to get away to bed, gladder still that Matthew did not know about the weaving, and that Shay was wining and dining a customer. He, after all, had already watched the pieces take shape and he had said nothing derogatory, though, come to think of it, he had not really said anything in commendation either.

Were they really so bad? She looked at them again, the gentle blues and the sunny yellow-golds. Surely Mr. Felgate-Winter could use them for little-girl A-line coats with button-down collars. Stop! Something was wrong. Her eyes dropping with weariness, she sat up in bed. Was the idea to *persuade* Mr. Felgate-Winter to buy, or to present him with a promotion and product that teamed like Gilbert and Sullivan? Colours and patterns that people would recognise without even spotting the arms-akimbo figure on the Young O'Malley badge. And suddenly she saw it—pastels were out, all along the line it had to be richness with off-beat twills and acid knops for contrast.

The cornfield perhaps with poppies, and laid on a rich background.

Would I like that myself? she thought doubtfully, for she'd always pictured putting herself into the fabrics. Again there was an answer. The professional did not back her own preference—she made an intelligent contribution to the master plan. Like a script-writer.

So! He thinks I can't do that, does he? That I'm not professional enough? Fuddy-duddy, if you please! I'll give him fuddy-duddy!

It was her last thought before sleep.

Next morning at breakfast Shay asked diffidently: "What about those pieces, love? Want me to show them to the boss?"

Johanna, with one eye on Clootie preparing to leap on to Shay's knee, and her head full of the new idea for the cornfield—a background of parma violet with a twill in corn and scarlet, answered lightly: "No, I quite like you in one piece! They were only starters. I've got more sense than to think they'd do for Young O'Malley."

Shay took out a new white handkerchief and slowly mopped his brow.

"Thank the lord for that, ducky," he said fervently. "I've been wondering all night how to tell you."

Douglas's lectures had ceased for the summer break and he was in and out for most of the day. Flann's deep bay of joy as they set out for a walk sounded more than once and from a vantage point on the balcony Johanna saw them up on the hill, silhouetted on the skyline, Flann rangy and lithe, his master trunky and, even from that distance, phlegmatic, monarch of all he surveyed.

She had only to look at him to blaze again. *Fuddy-duddy! Thinks I'm behind the times. Thinks I can't get the message. I'll show him. I'll give him fuddy-duddy!*

In a matter of hours her whole approach to Young O'Malley had changed. She'd even begun to see what Matthew O'Malley had found so frustrating in the first designs Shay had produced. They didn't fit the gay tearaway symbol, they didn't swing. Any more than her own had done up to now. But now, even on the drawing board, they had the sizzle of Myles's own colour schemes—another parma ground with a darting twill of green and fuchsia red, a peacock spiced with parma and yellow, and a vivid twill and tabby in purple, yellow, green and orange with a line of dragon red. Without the loom they couldn't, of course, be woven, but how silly that caper had been. Had she really seen herself dropping the tweed lengths negligently in front of Matthew O'Malley and saying: "Oh, just a thing or two I've been tying up!" You needn't laugh, she told herself, you really did, *you old fuddy-duddy!*

She knew better now; all she now aspired to be was one of the team.

Clootie's nose, in its way, was a thermometer. On a cool day it was the colour of a Malmaison carnation, on a warm one a Queen Elizabeth rose. At mealtimes excitement made it brighter still. Banned from the dining-room, he was always at the door watching a chance to dart in. Tonight he was absent.

"I wonder where he is," Johanna said.

"Perhaps he's gone to be a guinea-pig," Shay suggested hopefully.

Matthew said nothing. He had been quiet all day Johanna thought he might be in pain but was too shy to ask.

"Clootie! Clootie! Clootie!" she called.

"If it's the grey one," said Alice as though they'd half a dozen, "I saw Mr. Douglas with him."

Johanna paused sharply. No! He couldn't. Not without warning her, and not like that—grabbing a little thing when it was waiting for its dinner. But then he was a realist if ever there was one, and Clootie's future was as yet unspoken for.

She went down to the surgery, tapped perfunctorily on the door and entered.

Douglas in white coat was bending over something on the table, something which Ray, his student helper, was holding down. The something, held like a trussed rabbit, was Clootie. He rolled his eyes at Johanna, feebly, she thought.

"Clootie . . . you're not . . ." There was a slim silver instrument in Douglas's hand and instinctively she looked away.

"No choice," said Douglas. "Come in or stay out," he added ungallantly. "I don't want the door open."

Blindly she went out, shutting the door as requested.

Shay had gone out. His car had developed clutch trouble and he had taken it to be looked at. Matthew was sitting on the terrace. He made no sign of seeing Johanna as she approached and more than ever she felt that something was wrong. Instinct urged her to slip past quickly, something else inside her spoke differently. Was she to make a habit of running from trouble? "Mr. O'Malley, can I get you something?"

"Oh, it's you, Jo," he started. "Sit down."

She did so. "Ever feel you'd had it?" he asked suddenly.

The doctor had warned that the beneficial effect of the new tablets might wear off. It seemed this was happening. At her enquiry, however, Matthew shook his head. "It's not my joints. A moment of truth more like. Knocking on and not that much to show for it."

"Mr. O'Malley!" she gasped incredulously. He was still so young-looking, hardly a line on his face, just those wings of grey in his hair. Smart shirts were a thing with him, to-day's was hyacinth blue, in a heavy self-patterned fabric like damask. "You don't mean that, you couldn't. Look at O'Malley Tweeds."

"Yes," he said quietly, "I'm looking." There was a pause. "As a matter of fact I'm thinking of giving up." At her gasp he turned to her. "Oh, they'd be all right. I've had feelers put out for a merger."

Somehow they seemed to be talking as equals. "And you?" Johanna asked.

"Personally, out," he said simply. "There'd be a seat on the board for my wife, a guarantee of no redundancy, and a management post for Shay with a directorship in two years."

"But what would you do?"

"Go somewhere warm and dry. I can soak up as much sun as I'm given. Forget there's such a thing as the Irish climate." He gave her the swift boyish smile. It looked extremely forced. "Needs thinking about, of course, but I'm tempted."

If he were, she thought, it did not show in his face.

"Don't mention this to the boys," he added. "Douglas won't care, of course, but Shay will be upset."

She realised she had just happened along in the moment of truth, but as he had said this much she felt she could say some more. "He may not be directly concerned, Mr. O'Malley, but Douglas will care, I'm sure. He knows and cares about O'Malley Tweeds a great deal more than you may think. He——" Horrorstruck, she broke off. To say more would be to involve herself, the silly business of the loom and the patterns.

"Go on," Matthew bade with quickening interest.

The story came out—it had to; the colours he had selected, the effort he made to retain the loom for her, finally the criticisms. "They made me boil," she admitted. "But he knew what he was about."

Matthew listened silently. His: "Hm," at the end was puzzling.

"No matter," he said quickly when she questioned it. "Go and get me those designs. I can't think why you didn't come to me in the first place. I'll probably throw them out, mind," he called after her.

She still did not want to display them, least of all without Shay's backing, but the memory of that still figure in the luc blue shirt and knowing now the thoughts that had been his made it impossible to refuse. Not her business, of course, but how repugnant, how wrong, the idea of his retirement was.

The doctor had been so pleased with his progress of late, had said the arthritis could improve still further, and had stressed over and over again the importance of keeping up his interests. Shay had told her this and she remembered thinking back to one frightening time at home when her father had overturned a tractor and had been on his back for months. He had only got back on his feet by fighting every inch of the way, but then—her mother had fought alongside. Wasn't that the trouble here? Sheila O'Malley was as big a fighter as her husband, but they weren't on the same side.

At no other time had Knockbeg with all its loveliness seemed so hollow, its happiness so temporal, the odd laughing moments, even the trifling ones with a kitten were all doomed to end in tragedy. But there, she wouldn't think of Clootie, he was only a tiny cog in the wheel.

She gathered the designs together and hurried out. As

she closed the kitchen door behind her she saw Douglas crossing the lawn. He stopped and put something down on the grass. The something crouched for a second, then leaped forward like a frog. Hind legs like a rabbit, forelegs like a frisking lamb, Clootie remembering his dinner rushed excitedly to meet her.

Johanna rushed too; the little ungainly shape running home and released in her a fount of joy and gratitude. A life had been spared because she'd asked for it, it was the happiest nicest thing Douglas O'Malley could have done.

"Oh, thank you, thank you so much!" He was in her path, looking a little puzzled. She stopped on tiptoe and flung her arms round his neck. His head jerked back in astonishment: "What have I done to deserve this?"

A little chilled, she explained. "Clootie, of course."

"Thank you," he murmured politely. "I hope he feels as grateful. After all, I have cramped his style for him."

"You've done what?"

"You saw," he answered briefly. "I've just castrated him. He's probably going to end up with my godmother, She has about fifty cats as it is, but she's always helping me out. She won't look at him, though, unless that's been done. What's the matter?" He was staring at her face.

Matter? Everything. How like him to make her feel a fool!

"I thought you were putting him down."

"Putting him down? And how did you think I was doing it, for heaven's sake? With a scalpel?" Red-faced and embarrassed, she said nothing. "I don't know about you, young Jo." Eyes crinkled with amusement looked out at her from under the broad forehead. "You'll have to do a lot of homework before you're a vet's wife."

"I think that contingency is too remote to concern either of us," Johanna said haughtily."

Matthew looked keenly at the sketches and the rough pattern notes she'd made. Three more designs had now joined the first four, two of which she thought might in gossamer weight, do for shirts or dresses, one a peacock and strawberry draughtboard, purple where the threads crossed; the second a deep orange stripe effect that merged almost unnoticeably to yellow and dark red. The last one she fancied for a suit. It was a tabby weave in deep and dusty pinks and nasturtium with an odd touch of blue and red. He darted questions about weight, nodding quickly as she answered. It was impossible to be sure what he thought.

"That's my girl, they're marvellous!" Shay praised. "What do you think, sir?"

"Well, at least they're different." Matthew closed the folder. "I presume I may keep them. I'd like to look at them again in the morning."

"He didn't exactly enthuse, did he?" Johanna observed doubtfully when she was alone with Shay.

"If you ask me, love," Shay propounded, "he hadn't the breath for it. Mark my words, first thing tomorrow he'll be on to Harry. And then, again mark my words, some lucky girl should be in the money."

The words penetrated slowly. "In the money? You mean he might want to pay me?"

No "might" about it, Shay assured her. Pay well too, he added warmly. O'Malleys were very fair about that sort of thing.

It was another bridge to cross, a bothersome one. She couldn't possibly take money for the designs. They were themselves a payback. But how to explain, how possibly to explain?

Shay and she had a bet as to whether or not Matthew would summon Harry Blake in the morning. They both lost. Shay had left for town and Johanna was arranging a bowl of flowers in the kitchen when Douglas put his head round the door and asked if she would be around for the next hour or so. "Good," he said when she assented. "I'll switch my phone through. If there are any calls tell them I'll be back by midday. I'm just driving my father down to the nursing home."

Johanna's: "To the nursing home?" got out a fraction after Alice's: "He *never*!"

Douglas ignored Alice. He looked poker-faced. "Yes, it seems he's got hold of some designs he thinks she ought to see."

"Good heavens, tonight!" Alice exclaimed dramatically

when they were again alone. "Must be going to sell out. That's all I can think of."

Johanna, not quite brave enough to point out that she had not been asked to think of anything, snipped the stalk of a rose called "The Doctor."

"Don't mind that about designs," Alice continued. "The Lord Almighty would want to have done them before he'd go down and ask her opinion, the poor unfortunate."

"Yes, well, we'll just have to wait and see," Johanna rejoined much more calmly than she felt.

It was almost impossible to wait, and when Matthew did return he told her very little. He had, at times, a hard look to fathom, a sort of shutter closed across his face.

"Those sketches of yours, we think something can be made of them. With a good deal of work, of course. I'm telling Harry Blake to drop everything else and get cracking. Meantime, my wife would like to see you."

Sheila O'Malley, in a peacock blue housecoat, was out of bed and sitting by the window. A drake's tail of copper-coloured hair snicked forward at one temple. Her cheeks were fuller and had a pale rose glow. Anything less like Alice's "poor unfortunate" could hardly be imagined.

She greeted Johanna cordially. "Come in, Miss Dykes. Sit down. Any trouble finding the way?"

"No," Johanna explained after the first preliminaries. "Shay brought me. He's downstairs now." She had been hoping to be sent down for him, Shay having given a flat and monosyllabic refusal to come further.

Sheila O'Malley, however, seemed supremely unconcerned with Shay. Her: "Oh yes?" had a studiedly casual note. "Well," she continued, smiling, "you've turned out to be a dark horse, haven't you?"

The words sang in Johanna's ears. The blood rushed to her face. The whole room seemed for one ghastly second to pitch forward and rest at an angle.

"A great deal more in you than meets the eye." The cool voice went on amusedly. It changed. "Is anything wrong?"

Quite unable to speak, Johanna shook her head. In a mirror behind Sheila O'Malley's chair, her own reflection mocked the reply. It was only too plain that she was terrified out of her wits.

This side of the mirror Sheila O'Malley's brown eyes under their flaring dark amber brows regarded her quizzically. "Don't look so guilty, then! I'm not talking about your past, just your designs."

Johanna held on to herself, the room slowly returned to normal, she made herself smile. "I don't know if they're any good."

"There speaks my husband," Sheila laughed. "I suppose he's made you feel we're doing you a favour instead of the other way round. Rest assured, they're good. I hope you're salting us, are you?"

"Mrs. O'Malley, I couldn't take any money for them. Please."

"But, my dear child, of course you must be paid. Why ever not?"

Johanna decided there was after all only one line to take—the truth so far as it would go. "Because I wanted to feel I was helping, even just a little, and now it's more than that. I owe it to you for my carelessness over Smokey. Mrs. O'Malley, I'm terribly sorry. Were you dreadfully upset?" She searched the face, even more beautiful now with the bloom of restored health. It looked back at her, obviously moved but puzzled.

"Upset, yes, not dreadfully. It was quick and perhaps merciful, so don't think any more about that. And the other—why should you want to help? We're nothing to you, my son was nothing to you." The pause was hard to bear because of the shade of enquiry in it. Johanna clenched her hands and said nothing. "Forgive me for sounding suspicious, I do believe you. I just find it hard to understand."

"I just wanted to," was all Johanna could say.

"Then I suppose we must just thank you and say there aren't many of you left."

Nerves as well as relief loosened Johanna's tongue: "It was for Shay too. He was so anxious . . ."

"Yes, I'm sure he was," the voice cut in, ice-cool. Johanna started. "You said Shay was anxious, I said I was sure he was. He won't get a break like Young O'Malley again." The tone was quiet, but it put Johanna on guard.

Mentioning Shay had been a mistake. She would not do so again.

Sheila O'Malley at that moment was also regretful. "You know, Sheila," Noel Kerry, her doctor, friend as well as physician, had said in the first days of her illness, "there's a virtue in knowing when we're up against something we can't change. I don't think you can do a thing about this scheme of Matt's except hurt yourself. Am I right?" She supposed Matthew had told him about the Board Meeting at which she'd been outvoted, two to one.

She supposed too that Matthew's visit yesterday morning with the child's sketches had been one of his unpredictable olive branches. Matthew never lost, so he could afford these whimsies. A chance to save face; she'd had it before, quite as insincere and contrived as everything Matthew had ever done. But she'd taken it. It was now tacitly allowed that the appeal of the designs had removed her opposition to Young O'Malley.

And the designs had been charming, as charming as their young creator, to-day in a mid-thigh paisley dress mostly poinsettia red. All eyes, just as she had remembered her, and with the timid mouth that you saw on chocolate box kittens. Sheila O'Malley had never thought of a daughter, always sons, tall, dark, blade-slim. She could not tell why the thought should have wandered across her mind at just that moment unless it was that when she looked back at her visitor it was to see her staring as though mesmerized at Myles's photograph. That was another thing Noel Kerry had said: "You've got to bring Myles out, Sheila, and talk about him. If you don't, you really will have a breakdown. I'm telling you straight."

"Yes, that's Myles," she said stiffly. "Bring it over if you like. You'll see better. The child had quite long arms, narrow pointed fingers, pale oval-shaped nails. She held Myles's photograph very gently. "He was to have been Young O'Malley," Sheila said. "It was his idea, all of it. He had such vision, such drive. He would have made us world-famous. Not that that would matter if I had him . . ." she broke off, shocked at the emotional spate. In all the weeks since the accident she'd never spoken like this.

"Was he—killed outright?" The question was almost inaudible.

"So they assure me."

"Then he couldn't have known anything." The soft voice seemed to tremble. "I'm so glad."

"It was half my fault, you know." She had never got this into the open before. "He wrecked his car in London. My husband didn't want him to have another. But he was going on holiday to Scotland to fish. He said a car would make all the difference. So I lent him one. I've often asked myself what devil prompts us at times like that . . ."

"No, please," the voice begged. Johanna was staring at her with eyes like saucers. "Don't think of it like that. You can't see round every corner, and at least," she paused and looked down at the photograph in her hands. "At least you let your love go all the way."

"I don't know," Sheila said heavily. "These weeks I've realized just how little I do know. For instance, where he was really going that day. I know Douglas thinks . . ." she checked. Unburdening herself beyond the small charmed circle, which every year now was growing smaller, had always been virtually impossible. The fact that talking to this child seemed so unconscionably easy was no reason to continue.

Besides, there was something else. Frankly, a worry. She was torn. Not to let Gerry down, she was such a stand-by, worked so hard, a second right hand, and with it all in love and unsure. Any woman would sympathise. And Johanna Dykes was distractingly pretty. "Setting her cap at Douglas," Gerry had said. Well, she would have her work cut out, Douglas's mother had thought. Nonetheless some things should be said for the child's own sake. In fact, she had already said them to Douglas three weeks ago when she'd first learned of Johanna's appointment. "That child? You must be joking." Not a smile. How stolid Douglas could be! "If you'd put in as many advertisements as I have, Mother, without so much as a phone call, you wouldn't feel much like joking."

"Johanna," she said now, "if I may call you that— there is just one other thing. You *are* being careful?"

The huge eyes, trout stream brown, gazed back. *"Careful,* Mrs. O'Malley?"

"At home?" Sheila stressed gently. "With Douglas. I know my husband's there, and Alice most of the time, but you're so young and pretty I . . ." It was painful to watch the face now staring at her, flushed and aghast.

"Mrs. O'Malley, I . . ."

"Don't take this amiss, please. If I'd been home when I first thought I would be it would have been different, just a few days . . . though I did say to Douglas you seemed—very young. But now it's been three weeks and probably another one before I leave here. I feel I have to say it to you. It's so easy to start people talking and so embarrassing for all concerned, even if there's no cause, as I feel sure in your case there wouldn't be." She was sure there would be nothing intentionally out of line, but unintentionally was a different matter. The child was dynamite.

"Mrs. O'Malley, have there been any—complaints about me?" All rosiness had left the young round cheeks, they were ash pale and the eyes looked bigger than ever.

"Not complaints," Sheila said firmly. "Just a word or two from someone a bit better qualified to judge perhaps than you."

There was still hardly a vestige of colour in the face as its owner got to her feet. "I don't know what you've heard, Mrs. O'Malley, but it was a complete misunderstanding. I won't even say it won't occur again, it *couldn't.*"

"My dear child, I don't know what you're talk—" Sheila stopped as the door opened and one of the nurses looked in. The nurse said quickly: "Sorry, I'll come back," but Johanna seized the opportunity.

"No, please, I must go. I mustn't keep Shay waiting any longer."


"Did she say anything about Myles?" Alice asked avidly as she stirred the teapot. "I liked Myles. More fun in him than Douglas."

Clootie's antimacassar-like body, thick, strong and warm, was comforting to hold on to. Alice fortunately, Johanna realized, had attributed her looks to Sheila O'Malley discussing Smokey's death.

"Did she give out to you, ducky? What did you say?" The kettle was on and she made tea, reverting to the tragedy of Myles. "God love her, all the same though, it's a terrible cross. To be taken like that before he'd even got started. And that's thanks to him in there." She nodded sagely in the direction of Matthew's study.

"Heard them at it hammer and tongs one day. She wanted Myles made a director and he said no, not till he was twenty-five, and then young Shay would have to be made one too. Well, she wouldn't have that at all, and would you blame her? Proper little upstart that bucko, and well named."

"Shay?" Johanna echoed, trapped in spite of herself.

"Oh, you wouldn't know, o' course," Alice allowed graciously. "In English it'ud be James, and that's the same as Jacob 'the supplanter'. It's in me list of names outa' the magazine I gets. Couldn't be much truer, could it?" she challenged.

"I don't know what you're talking about, Alice," Johanna said firmly. "Or why you should think Mrs. O'Malley doesn't like Mr. Shay."

As soon as uttered she knew the statement was a mistake. It called for contradiction and it got it. A dark colour suffused Alice's nose, bringing it, it seemed, to bursting point.

"Don't you really, miss?" she demanded, bridling. "Well, I don't know what you've got eyes for, then, that's all!" Angrily, she stumped away from the table.


CHAPTER TEN

NEXT week Shay was back in Donegal and Douglas doing locum for a friend on holiday. This with his own practice meant that Knockbeg hardly saw him. Matthew had two bad days and distressed Johanna by announcing that he was going down by taxi to O'Malley House for further consultations about Young O'Malley. Shay was not there to be appealed to, Douglas she would not approach, so in the end she telephoned Harry Blake herself and requested him to move the meeting to Knockbeg. Unfortunately, Matthew took this as an infringement of rights.

"I make the decisions," he barked. "It's for me to say what I'll do."

"It's for me to say," he repeated roughly and resentfully, and then abruptly gave in: "All right. Organize coffee or something when they come."

He had not referred again to the merger, and Young O'Malley was obviously going ahead by leaps and bounds, but this need only be expansion to attract a better bid.

It was hard to realize that in approximately a fortnight she would see no more of the O'Malleys. Sheila was expected home next Sunday and Matthew had referred briefly to the end of August as being a suitable deadline for the household to return to normal.

"Though I hope we may continue to do business. Show us anything you've got on the stocks. We may not take them, of course, but no harm done."

"In other words," Shay interpreted with a grin when he and Johanna were alone, "we're dead keen."

At about half past four on Friday afternoon Johanna went into Sheila O'Malley's bedroom to make sure that it was ready for Sunday. The inspection was unnecessary. Alice, whatever about her slanders, was one hundred per cent efficient in her work. The room with its striking colour scheme of dark blue walls, gold ceiling and brilliant white furniture was spotless and she was closing its door again when Douglas walked out of the kitchen.

"Hullo there," he said easily. "Any sign of Shay?"

"No. Mr. O'Malley, you know he's in Donegal," Johanna answered smoothly.

The brows lifted slightly. "What's all this, then? Why are we being so formal?"

"I just thought—we can't be too careful."

"Oh yes?" His head had gone drolly to one side. She looked away. In the past when he had done that it had always been rather warming.

"Did you want Shay, Mr. O'Malley?"

"No, no, just interested," he replied enigmatically, and sauntered off again, hands in his pockets.

A short time later Shay's yellow car bounded up the drive and a few minutes after that Shay opened the kitchen door, somewhat clumsily because of the covered basket one hand was carrying.

111

"What have you got?" Johanna asked curiously.

"This you'll not believe, darling," Shay returned, "but I have driven one hundred and fifty miles with *that* in the car with me." He put the basket on the table. "There you are, love, compliments of the house!"

A squeak for all the world like a cracker toy sent Johanna's fingers fumbling with the hasp. The lid came up and with it, quite negligently, a slim gold paw. Inside, and smiling up at her from a peacock-blue blanket, was a ball of red-gold kitten. An aristocrat, she saw at once, from its neat well-pricked ears to its tiny pansy face and the cream and amber tail which looked a bit like plastic foam.

"For me?" She lifted the soft silky body and put it against her cheek. It squeaked again and cuddled into her, a little lion in the making.

"Who else?"

"Oh, Shay!" She put the kitten down and flung her arms round his neck. He did not look in the least taken aback and he kissed her roundly in return. "Where did you get him? He's perfect!"

He was, he had all his points, small wide face, short legs, cobby body, and what a colour! From deep flame on his back he merged on belly, paws and tail into amber and cream.

"Where *did* you get him?" Johanna repeated ecstatically.

"Confession is good for the soul, *I* didn't," Shay said, backing away. "I'm just the taximan. Douglas got it from his godmother. She lives in Carrickdoo."

Douglas had to be thanked. He opened the door in checked shirt sleeves with a tumbler of milk in one hand. "Oh, come in. Just excuse me getting on with this, will you? I haven't time for dinner tonight." He looked at her gravely, said: "*Slainte*," and put the glass to his lips.

Johanna found herself struggling with a dangerous wave of tenderness. She controlled it sternly. Not for diamonds would she risk another rebuff.

"No, I won't come in, thanks," she said sedately. "I just wanted to say thank you for the kitten. I—I'm absolutely delighted. He's beautiful." Somehow the words lacked punch. She had been able to thank Shay so much better for his part.

"That's all right. Glad he's up to specification." He stood there looking at her, uncertainly she felt. "I haven't seen him myself yet."

"I'll bring him up if you like."

The dark head shook and its owner took a further hasty swig. " 'Fraid not. I'm dashing."

"Was your godmother looking for a home for him?"

"Er—yes—she—er—always has dozens. I told you that." He straightened the knot of his tie and grabbed bag and jacket.

For all its delicate looks the kitten was a buffoon. It jumped on shoulders and unwary backs and it had a smirk of a mouth. Clootie, however, saw little to smirk about. He put up his back like a porcupine and backed away spitting. Douglas carried him in from the garden, his geisha eyes pools of sadness.

"Feels insecure," Douglas explained.

"Oh, did you have to?" Johanna sighed. "He's so rough."

To prove her words, Clootie darted wickedly at the new addition, bowled him over and held him in a clinch. The dainty salmon pink pads kicked futilely and their owner squealed.

"Naughty Clootie!" cried Johanna with a smack to the white shoulders.

She looked up to see a strange expression on Douglas's face and back down again in time to notice that one of the aggressor's almond green eyes had been accurately dotted by a toy-like golden paw.

"What'll you call him? Ginger?" Alice asked.

It was an insult. The name had to mean something. She said so and Alice beamed. "I'll bring in my buke tomorrow."

It was from Alice's "buke" that the kitten was finally named, "Ken", because it was Celtic and because it meant "handsome". He learned it in two days and squeaked happily in answer. Johanna learned something else under the pretext of looking up her own name, though it was regrettable that Alice should notice her eyes lingering over long in the "D" section. Alice missed nothing. "If it's Douglas you're looking for," she said kindly, "it means 'dark grey'. Colour of his eyes," she added.

"Grand little one, isn't she?" Alice remarked to the company at large as she set down a blue and white dish of curry in front of her mistress.

"She is indeed," Sheila O'Malley agreed. "I don't know where we'd all have been without her." She smiled warmly at Johanna. It was a good moment and a fitting culmination to the day's labours.

Alice had told her that Sheila O'Malley liked curry, so she had chosen it for this first night home supper and served it with all the side effects the cookery book had recommended—banana in lemon juice, cucumber and soured cream and cooked pineapple with almonds. She had used the prettiest dishes she could find, basketwork for the rolls, earth red for the banana, gleaming stainless steel for the cucumber with its dusting of paprika, and she had made a centrepiece of the vivid dahlias which were now coming into their own in the garden.

Douglas and Geraldine had joined them and Alice had insisted on coming in, though normally she did not do so on Sunday. She had even dressed for the occasion in startling royal blue with a silver trim.

The meal had got off to a good start, Sheila at one end of the oval table, slim, flame-topped, gracious, in champagne-coloured nylon, a thin shirt-dress with long sleeves, and facing her, Matthew, for once with a jacket on and looking particularly handsome in its grey flannel suiting. He had not exactly said: "Good to have you home, my dear" when his wife, with Douglas carrying her case, had come into the hall, but at least he had been there.

"Matthew," Sheila had said, and they'd looked at each other quietly, appraisingly.

Now, however, Johanna realized with some dismay that the spotlight was being thrown on her, for Matthew was lifting his glass:

"Ladies and gentlemen, Johanna—our designing housekeeper!"

"Johanna," they echoed, and drank.

A moment heady, glowing—and galling. To look at Douglas no one would imagine that he considered his father's pun anything but a joke, and yet he had found it necessary to safeguard himself against any designs she might have had in mind.

As the meal proceeded the talk turned to "shop", the retrospective wage award which Shay had finally agreed last week with the union representatives, and naturally the progress of Young O'Malley. If it hurt Sheila to learn that Matthew was seeking an appointment for Shay with Mr. Felgate-Winter to submit cloths for approval, she gave no sign of it, and, watching her quick response to the various points, Johanna's heart went out in admiration of her control and courage. And then, quite suddenly, the picture changed. Sheila O'Malley leaned towards the side of the table at which Shay was seated.

"And when you get back from London, Shay, perhaps you'll find time for flat-hunting."

Shay's eyes changed, but not his good-humoured countenance "Will do, Mrs. O'Malley. You've been very patient."

In the same breath Matthew cut in: "What does Shay want a flat for? We've agreed his home is here."

"That's your opinion," Sheila said coolly.

The impact was instantaneous and universal. Douglas clinked down his glass, Geraldine's cheeks reddened quite amazingly, Shay swallowed. Matthew, his eyes under their long black lashes bright and almost venomous, jerked in his seat: "And what do you mean by that?"

"Heavens, Matthew, don't get so hot under the collar," Sheila reproved composedly. "I'm only thinking of Shay and the disadvantages of living on the job. You must realize that you never give him a moment's peace."

"He can always come to me," Matthew began to stutter. "Put his case. Complain. He knows he'll get a hearing. People can always come to me. It's what I'm here for."

"Yes, it's all right, sir," Shay put in. "I'm not complaining."

"See?" Matthew's head jerked.

"Well then," Sheila said, still smiling, "perhaps I am. Just a little. If I could get the right sort of help here, I daresay it would be easier . . ."

"Mother," Douglas interposed, "do we have to go into all this now?"

"Of course not," his mother said pleasantly. "I just want Shay to bear it in mind."

"And I'd like *you* to bear something in mind." Matthew, with a blazing look, snatched the words out of her mouth. "It's this. I make the decisions. I want Shay, he stays. I can't do without him. When I can we'll talk about his going. Is that understood?" The harsh voice smote Johanna's ears with almost physical force.

Sheila O'Malley looked singularly untouched. These two would never mix, Johanna thought wearily, they were like fire and water. And she remembered suddenly that in the end water quenched fire.

Shay had a habit of leaving towels in the little changing pavilion at the swimming pool and after supper Johanna, turning her thoughts to the more mundane topic of tomorrow's wash, went on her weekly round-up. She was about to enter the pavilion when she heard Geraldine's voice inside it.

"You're a fool, Shay. You should get out."

Johanna stepped firmly on to the brick threshold. "Any towels in there?"

"Oh, come in, Jo," Geraldine answered easily. "Yes— take your pick!"

She and Shay were standing looking at each other.

"I wouldn't like you to think I was eavesdropping," Johanna said warily.

"No matter," Geraldine said carelessly. "I was just telling Shay that in my opinion he ought to look for another job."

Another job! It was so revolutionary a thought that Johanna found herself staring stupidly. Geraldine had always been an unknown quantity. This evening, however, there seemed to be no pretence about her.

"I'm perfectly serious. You heard what happened just now. It's an intolerable position. They're like two dogs fighting over a bone."

"A tough bone," Shay said, smiling.

Johanna looked from one to the other, shocked and uncertain. Her eyes stayed on Geraldine. "But what would happen to Young O'Malley?"

"Something," Geraldine asserted lightly, "would turn up. And don't look at me as though I ought to be heading for Traitor's Gate. I've watched those two hurt each other for years. It's a darn shame, because she's not a bit like that really. But I can't stomach . . ." She broke off sharply, looking back to Shay. "Well, it's up to you, of course," she finished, and went out.

She left silence behind her. Shay, with a hand on the doorpost, stood gazing after her tall slight figure, not in the crios dress to-day, but in fuchsia pink crimplene, with her hair caught on top by a flat ribbon bow. Johanna with one of the towels on her arm stood watching Shay. His slacks matched his shirt and his lightweight tweed jacket repeated the gold in its cheeks. He looked troubled, as well he might.

"She's really concerned about you," Johanna said softly. "I saw her face at supper." He shrugged, saying nothing. "*Would* you leave?" she pressed.

"No. Not unless they kick me out."

"I'm not sure she's not right. You could easily get another job." He shrugged again. "Shay, have you had offers?"

"Maybe." Plainly he would say no more and, plainly, she had no right to expect it. She found a second towel and was making for the door when he spoke.

"Jo. How about getting married?"

"Getting married?" She stood staring. "You mean— you and me?"

"Yes, love," he answered simply. "Getting married and finding a place of our own . . ."

"You mean . . ." she tried to make it a joke, "get married so as you have a reason for moving out of Knockbeg without offending Matthew?"

The dark eyes flickered as Shay came across, took her hands and swung them gently. "No, darling, that's not what I mean, as you very well know. I mean a whole lot of things that I hardly know how to say. I did take a toss over Gerry, I'll admit, a bad one, but the moment I saw you something else happened to me." His hands left hers and went, still gently, up her arms to her shoulders. "Something very nice," he added softly.

She let him fondle her, towel and all. Such a dear,

117

straightforward, loyal and unselfish. His role in O'Malley Tweeds was at times intolerable, he never complained, but at that moment it was in his face. Things would be better if there were no question of his living on the job and perhaps as his wife she herself could do something to help. At any rate she could design.

If Shay could accept that Geraldine was the fruit out of his reach then, with even less questioning, she must accept that Douglas—but she would not so much as frame such a ridiculous thought.

"Oh, Shay," she said breathlessly, "it was very nice for me too."

"Then what about it, love?" He was in earnest. She didn't know whether she wanted him to be or not, but it was touching and sweet. "I do care for you and we could be happy, I know it. We like all the same things."

"What about Ken?" she teased.

"I went a hundred and fifty miles with him, didn't I?" Shay pointed out. "You're going to say no," he said a few seconds later. "I thought you would."

"No," she said quickly. "Nor yes, either," as his face lit. "Just let me think about it."

"You think too much, Jo," he told her sadly. "I don't know whether you know it or not, but you're always going away from us with that chap you lost."

"Oh no! I do think about Myles, but not like . . ." she stopped. Shay was staring at her, round-eyed with astonishment.

"Myles? *Myles? Myles who?*"

For a king's ransom she couldn't have answered. Sick and incredulous of herself, she stood gazing back. How could she, how could she have let it slip? Now of all times when less than a fortnight remained of her secret mission. And now . . . Now Shay gathered her comfortingly close. She stood trembling. No need to say: "Myles O'Malley." He had guessed.

"Tell me about it."

"I can't."

"You must, darling. It will help." He kicked forward a chair, sat down and took her on to his knee. "Were you and Myles . . ."

"Oh no! No, we weren't." Even as she said the words

118

they mocked her. What had Myles really intended to happen in Edinburgh? What really had made her hesitate and change her mind? In her heart of hearts did she not know? The answer was yes. It had been inside her for quite a long time. "We were going to be married," she asserted doggedly. "In Scotland. I was the one he was meeting." Her change of heart and the reason behind the telephone call from Norwich did not seem worth mentioning. She left them out as she half-sobbed the rest of the story. "You won't tell, Shay? Promise. No one knows, not even my parents. Promise you won't tell." Her voice rose hysterically.

"Of course I won't tell," Shay soothed, still holding her. "You can trust me, Jo. I swear it."

It must have been half an hour before she felt able to go back to the house.

"And us, love?" Shay questioned softly as they crossed the lawn. "How long will you be with your thinking?" It was said half jestingly and very appealingly.

"Not too long," Johanna promised.

"I wonder." Shay stopped suddenly and looked at her. "I've had no leave this year. What say I ask Matt for a few days and take you to Carrickdoo? No strings," he added. "It's just a good place to think in—Carrickdoo."

It had been arranged that Johanna should travel home on Monday the first of September and Matthew anticipated that Shay would be going to London the same week. With amazing docility he agreed to the Carrickdoo trip the week before. "Tuesday or Wednesday," he promised vaguely. "We'll see how things go." Johanna, with a thought for the tourist season, mentioned to Shay that such vagueness did not make it easy for her to book a hotel room, but he retorted at once: "Who said anything about a hotel? We're staying with my mother.'

"But will that be all right?" Johanna murmured, somewhat taken aback.

"Oh yes, she'll be there for another few weeks," Shay answered carelessly. "She does a bit across the water, but she's on holiday at present. There's not a whole lot for her in Carrickdoo," he explained, "so when she got us off her hands she went back."

It was a little confusing, but Johanna knew that England was full of Irish workers, so why not a widow from Donegal? Shay's two sisters were also away from home, one married, one nursing. "By the way, my mother's a Catholic," he threw in casually. "And so are the girls. That's how I get hold of Saint Anthony so easily. I'm not one myself and my father wasn't. Again Johanna had the feeling that the information was not being thrown her as casually as it seemed. Shay was in fact assuring her that religion need be no bar to their marriage.

It was a quiet week, her second last in Knockbeg. Shay went to Donegal in the middle of it, partly to arrange for the making up of the wage award. There were no more scenes in public between Matthew and his wife and since Geraldine was on leave Sheila insisted on spending some time each day in O'Malley House. It was quite true that on her own she was a different person, not above giving a hand in the kitchen and disarmingly taken with Ken. "I shall miss him when he goes," she said laughingly. "We're a colour match, aren't we?" Sitting with Ken in a flame ball on her lap it was amazingly true.

"I shall miss you too, Jo," Sheila said another day. "So much."

The week's main enlivement was the kittens. They grew almost hourly, Ken's short scurrying legs giving an impression of anxiety which was totally misleading. Nothing went wrong for Ken, he was the sunniest of cats. Clootie was the fusser. Would he get to his plate before it was given to another? Were they still there—his people that he bossed around? Curled in sleep, he would often open a green "boiled sweet" eye to check.

"Thinks it's too good to be true," Douglas commented. "He's lost two homes already, remember."

And was going to lose this one, Johanna remembered, and pushed the thought away. She was sure Douglas's godmother would be kind to him, but in his thieving graceless way Clootie seemed to have taken to this household. Now both eyes were open and fixed on Douglas who had taken a pencil from his pocket and was making it draw circles in the air.

"I'm not busy tonight," Douglas observed. "So if

you want your chap castrated I could do him."

Johanna looked tremulously at Ken's "fox cub" face with its puffy cheeks and bright pink lips. "All right, but I'd better come too."

"Fine," said Douglas easily. "I don't think Linda could manage four legs on her own."

Linda Gibson, he explained, as they went down the drive, was helping him out during her school holidays and when they entered the surgery the tall teenager who owned the chocolate-eating poodle was there.

"Linda, Johanna, Ken," Douglas introduced them. He always said "Ken" as though it were a joke. "Sure you'll be all right?" he added in a low tone to Johanna. "I don't want you doing a die on me."

She nodded, firmly taking Ken's back legs as Linda grasped the front ones. As a game, it struck Ken as poor. He made a reedlike protest and Johanna caught her breath.

Johanna had not realized what it entailed; injections were all right, not blood, she couldn't look at blood. Desperately she closed her eyes and opened them again as the wound, so small she could hardly see it, was being swabbed and disinfected. A last injection against infection, this time in the scruff of Ken's blazing gold neck, and then Douglas was saying: "Right. There may be a drop or two of blood, but don't worry. He'll be fine."

Johanna straightened, but the room did not. It went on going round, and her head buzzed.

"Golly, you look queer!" Linda's blue eyes were fixed on her. "Are you going to faint?"

She didn't have to answer. An arm more efficient than gentle seized her and guided her to a chair and a hand like a sledge-hammer forced her head down between her knees. Unasked, Linda, whose efficiency made Johanna feel worse than ever, brought a glass of water.

When she had gulped the contents of this Johanna felt better, but Douglas would not hear of her standing up. It was five minutes past the end of surgery hours and Linda was tidying up. "That's all right. Thanks. I'll do the rest," Douglas said to her.

"I must go too," Johanna began. It would never do to sit on here alone with him, not after what he'd said. *So easy to start people talking and so embarrassing when they do.* She wriggled to the chair edge, her eyes now resting concernedly on Ken, who was crouching on the table with his back to her and his long brush of a tail flat out.

"Sit!" commanded Douglas as though she were Flann.

"What *is* the trouble?" he demanded when Linda had gone bicycling down the drive. "I'm not going to eat you."

"I don't want to cause talk," Johanna blurted.

"Talk? You mean because we've let the chaperone go?"

She nodded.

"May I ask what you have in mind?" She realized uncertainly that there was no amusement in his voice. "My dear child," he continued, "you're the one who has the designs, let's be quite clear about me. I haven't one in my head, particularly not on someone half my age who . . ."

"Half of thirty-three is sixteen and a half," Johanna flashed. It was the first thing she thought of.

"I stand corrected," Douglas said, less steelily. "And I hope you do too. "Yes, I'm sorry," she faltered. It was unfair, suspiciously like *Heads I win, tails you lose,* but something about those dark grey eyes compelled the apology.

"And so you jolly well ought to be," their owner retorted. "Age apart, I do know better than to make passes at someone else's girl."

Johanna knew a second of panic. Did it look that way to everyone in Knockbeg? And *did she want it to?*

"Come on now, all friends here." The grey eyes teased. "I know what I usually mean when I bring a girl home. So I expect would you."

Yes, she thought, and if the moon turned blue at the same time she wouldn't be surprised. Douglas, however, was continuing: "If it's any good to you, you have my blessing." He picked Ken up and scratched him under the chin.

"So that's it, I'm afraid," Shay concluded. "I did my darnedest to switch it, but I can't." It was the following Monday, the day before he and Johanna were due to go to Carrickdoo. Instead, there had been a phone call from London asking him to bring forward his meeting with Mr. Felgate-Winter and his team as they would shortly be leaving for South America.

If the order went through it would be the biggest export deal O'Malley Tweeds had ever landed. In the circumstances, personal disappointment could not be allowed to show.

"Don't worry," Johanna assured. "I can see Carrickdoo another time."

"That's where you're wrong, love," Shay said, grinning. "It's all laid on and if I can possibly get through before Friday I'll join you. Doubt if I will, though. We've a whale of a lot to do." He sighed.

"We?"

"Oh yes, Gerry's flying over tomorrow to keep me right on the paper work." He said it quickly and added a reassurance. "Look, not to worry. That's all over. I wouldn't have her if I wasn't sure. Or let you go if I wasn't just as sure of the guy you're going with."

A dire suspicion was forming in Johanna's mind. "You don't mean . . ."

"That I asked Doug. Right first time."

Disappointment she could hide, but this was too much. She could imagine no greater strain than going to Donegal with Douglas. The last debacle in a list that seemed almost legion had been her near-faint last Thursday. In just that one small thing she'd wanted to prove herself, but as always she had failed. Every one of her dealings with Douglas O'Malley had shown her up as a weakling, how he must despise her. And now Shay was putting her under a compliment to him. It made a writhing addition to the other unrestful thoughts.

Shay, however, feverishly throwing things into a suitcase, saw nothing amiss.

"He made no bones, Jo. In fact he said it was a chance to bring Kate Martin that kitten."

# CHAPTER ELEVEN

"ALL the best, don't let Geraldine lose the laundry list," said Douglas laconically, and stepped back.

"Ta very much, will do," Shay returned. He kissed Johanna. "See you love, and remember, tomorrow don't speak to the man at the wheel!"

Over her round brown head he looked at the man in question. "Thanks again, Doug. What would we do without you?"

Douglas knew he had a niche, so had a long case clock. But he was glad to help. His father pushed Shay unmercifully.

Here in Dun Laoghaire where they had dropped Shay for the boat it was a pleasant evening, warm, still, and across the bar only a skin like oiled silk distinguished the dove-blue sea from the dove-blue sky. The berthed steamer had her port and starboard lights on. They glowed ruby and emerald in the light dusk. Quite a romantic scene, Douglas thought, and was glad that as yet no one had found out how to expose thoughts.

"Would you like to walk down the pier?" he suggested. "We could see her out."

No one had yet discovered a way of throwing thoughts up on a radar screen, but none the less you could sometimes see them. Johanna's akward hesitation was one of the times. Hang it, why isn't she at ease with me? he thought. Does she think I'm going to throw her into the sea?

With a couple of strident blasts from its hooter the boat announced its departure. Passengers waved frantically from the deck and Johanna, spotting Shay amongst them, waved furiously back.

"Could he not get on a plane?" she asked.

"He didn't try. He hates flying. Scares him rigid," Douglas answered. "Geraldine's the opposite. She's flying over in the morning." He looked thoughtfully at his companion. "I'm as sorry about this as you are, but it can't be helped."

She looked at him with those great Java-shaped eyes.

124

"I don't want you to feel you must go on my account."

"No, no, no, I'm not," he said hastily. "My father wants me to look into one or two things at the factory, and there's a good friend of my own in Carrickdoo whom I could well use a talk with. No, no, it's not you, so you can stop feeling guilty." She smiled hesitantly. "And there's another thing would help," he continued. "And that is if we buried the hatchet." This had gone home. He saw her flush. "Not that I'm really sure what it's all about," he paused for her to elucidate. She didn't, so he pressed on, "But we do seem fated to get the wrong side of each other. I suppose it's in the stars! We're going to spend a lot of the next few days in each other's company. Let's try to behave like two sane and sensible people. Brother and sister, if you like. After all, I was nearly your brother-in-law."

He had to put a hand to her elbow. She stopped so abruptly in her stride. *"My brother-in-law?"*

He looked deeply into the clear brown eyes, sending them, he hoped, a message. "Don't be frightened. Nothing will ever happen to you while I'm around."

"You thought Shay was my brother, remember. And I saw how it was between you right from the start."

"Oh yes, Shay," Johanna was murmuring. "Of course." She added like a child: "Do you know his mother? I've been wondering about staying with her. Will she want me?"

"Oh yes," Douglas assured. "Have no fears about Maire O'Malley. She's a charming, delightful person. But I'm afraid she won't get you. In the altered circumstances I thought it would be better if you came home with me."

And may they slit my tongue, he thought, before I tell anyone why. The old Irish saying: "I'd like to show you to my roses" transposed "I'd like to show you to Kate". For fifty-one and a half weeks of the year he was sensible, hardworking and dull. For one half week—well, he thought, for one half week, why should I wake up?

"No objections, I hope?" he asked casually. "I've cleared the point with Maire and Shay."

"No. No objections," Johanna said at once. "I'm very glad really. I'd like to see Clootie settling down."

"And no objections to the rest of the speech?"

"Good gracious no," she said briskly. "I've always wanted a brother. I should have had one, but he died when he was a baby."

"Fine," Douglas rejoined, and wondered need she have been quite so hearty.

Next morning he arrived early with the lidded basket and both kittens hopped joyfully inside. Ken, lifted out and still feeling the need for self-expression, dabbed a spoon-like paw at the milk jug. If he had not looked so lordly or his round golden eyes so interested, the resulting rivulets might not have been so annoying.

Johanna, mopping up, tried not to see a nearly white nose pressed to the basket fastening. "You'll be all right," she assured it. "You'll love it in Donegal. You'll have lots to play with."

She did not say good-bye to Ken who anyway was busy, whirling round Alice like a dervish and leaping for the strings of her apron. In the basket Clootie screamed for mercy. "Glad to see the back of that row," Alice remarked, and for a moment Johanna almost hated her.

The route lay north-west in a gentle curve and the first stop of any length was in Carrick-on-Shannon. The town was a charter boat centre and the river alive with cabin cruisers and people making them ready. Looking down from the four-span bridge the scene was gay, green park, white-railed landing stage and the broad river wearing its motley of red or turquoise hull and white or yellow cabin.

"Tired?" Douglas asked as they passed the sign which told them they were nearing Bundoran.

Johanna shook her head. The hours had passed all too swiftly, but she would never forget them or the man who had brought it all to life. The road they had travelled would always be inseparable from him.

Bundoran brought her first sight of the dark blue Atlantic with, northwards across the bay, the hills of Donegal. It also showed her a Flann turned puppy again as he slithered madly over the flat limestone rocks.

"O'Donnell country," said Douglas, giving her a helping hand on Aughrus Head. "Come on now. You should

126

see the Fairy Bridges. They're quite famous." He stretched out his hand. "Better hold on to me. Shay won't thank me if you take a header!"

She was glad to. An all-round weakling, she thought disparagingly, she hadn't a good head for heights, and gazing through the arches of rock at the waves foaming and booming in the caverns below the cliff had a hypnotic effect.

"It's all right. I won't let you go," Douglas said, and suddenly the simple remark took on a deeper meaning.

This was a man you could not doubt, any more than you doubted that day would follow night This was a man so strong that you could give him your life to hold as easily as your hand If it had been this man she'd promised to meet in Edinburgh nothing her father said would have turned her back.

*If it had been Douglas . . . Douglas instead of Myles.*

It was as simple as that, the fruit of four complex weeks. She'd groped and smarted and been all at sixes and sevens. But now she *knew*. Love had to be more than physical attraction or boy-and-girl fondness. It had to be strong, stable, demanding and wholly satisfying. It was why you tried to do things that you'd never done before. It was why you remembered things like a look and a shoulder against your own, and why a hand round yours felt so good.

It was also just about the most senseless thing she could have done—fallen in love with the man from whom fate barred her, and who, in any case, only wanted to be her brother.

"Are you cold?" Douglas asked, and she realised that she had shivered. "Anyway, it's time we were moving."

As they left first Bundoran and then the town of Donegal, the real Donegal country came to meet them with each mile, whitewashed cottages, often thatched, stone walls, hillsides freckled with gorse, coarse leys like tufted rugs and sea. All the colours were bold, grey, moss green, old gold, black and dark blue.

Unexpectedly, the car stopped on a rise and Douglas pointed to a cluster of roofs and a church spire down in a hollow. "There! That's Carrickdoo."

It lay, very small, at the head of Carrick Pass; and

Carrick Pass seven hundred feet down on the left-hand side of the car seemed to be no more than a sheep track.

They drove on over a bridge spanning a sparkling little river.

The village was mostly grey stone and whitewash. There was a memorial of some kind behind railings, a stone water trough and excitingly a sign with an arrow saying: O'MALLEY TWEEDS LIMITED. Disappointingly, Douglas ignored this. He drove straight down the main street, looking content and talking.

"The friend I told you about lives up there." He pointed to a branching road. "Vincent O'Neill. He's a vet. Semi-retired, spends most of his time doing research. I don't know if you'll see him. He's a loner, hardly ever goes out these days, Kate says. Pity. He's got something in his fingers that no amount of study can bring—healing." It was not difficult to gather that Vincent O'Neill had influenced him in his own choice of career.

"I'd like to meet him," Johanna said warmly.

"Yes, well, I'm afraid it won't be possible." Douglas seemed to have regretted having spoken. "He fights very shy of strangers. Times he doesn't even answer the telephone." He turned again and drove for about a mile. Ahead were grey stone gateposts and double gates standing open. "Keep your eyes skinned, for heaven's sake. I don't want to start by running over any of Kate's cats," he warned with a grin, and took the wide car neatly through.

She thought he was joking, but as the car went up the drive two black cats streaked across its bow. "See what I mean?" Douglas chuckled. "The look-out boys!"

Seconds later the drive opened into a gravel sweep. The house, a gem of Palladian architecture, was there and so were the cats. She counted seven and at just that moment a crescent of cream on the limb of a sycamore dropped to the ground and made eight.

Douglas touched the horn and at once the hall door opened and three barking dogs rushed down the steps. Behind them, also running, came a figure in a blue-green printed dress, a surprisingly girlish figure with flying slender legs and short curly hair. Douglas, first out of the car, was promptly enveloped by fawning dogs and slim hugging arms. Johanna, following shyly, noted that he seemed to be enjoying it immensely.

Douglas's eye was now upon her, his finger crooked. "Well, Kate, what do you think? Never mind the smut on her nose. We'll see she washes for tea!"

Close to, Kate was not as young as her shape. Her face was lined, especially round the deep-set blue-green eyes and her hair was greying. In looks and style she wasn't a patch on Sheila O'Malley, but she'd had the makings and it still showed in her smile. About fifty-two, Johanna decided, but young. At seventy she'd still be young, and in that lay debit as well as credit. Presiding at the tea-table she was quite vague, lifting covered dishes with an exploratory air and making it plain that all such things were Cook's concern alone. She had a cook, a housemaid and a general factotum (male). He closed the double doors carefully when the feline part of the retinue tried to follow into the beautiful light green and white dining-room with its Adam fireplace and over it, so appropriately, a reproduction of Jan Breughel's *Garden of Eden*.

Knockbeg for all its charm had a functional air and all its occupants gave an impression of drive and strength. Kate Martin's house seemed to lie in a charmed circle and Kate, surreptitiously smuggling tidbits to the dogs under the table, gave an impression only of fun.

The evening that followed was leisurely, a stroll in the grounds, dinner and an hour with the record player and Kate's rather sentimental favourites. Johanna, going sleepily to bed, left Douglas and his godmother still up. She was talking nineteen to the dozen; he, dug comfortably into a corner of the couch, was listening with one hand stroking his cheek. A habitual pose and an ordinary enough scene, but Johanna could not recall ever having seen anything like it in Knockbeg. It was illuminating and somehow infinitely touching.

## CHAPTER TWELVE

NEXT morning Johanna was up early and at her bedroom window. Kate's grounds marked the boundary between the village of Carrickdoo and the wild sea coast. On the lee side the coarse pasturelands, in the changing light, were lime, daffodil and gold. There was the splash of a white cottage, haystacks, a field of ripe wheat and the light-foliaged trees she'd noticed yesterday. On the side that marched out to meet the bay dark slate cliffs sharpened against the blanching sky.

The clip-clop of a horse's hooves roused her and she looked down to see a dark chestnut being walked up the drive. Astride it, in a blue Aran sweater, was Douglas. He saw her and waved: "Hullo there! Had breakfast?" She shook her head and he called again: "Well, shake a leg then, or you'll be unlucky!" Very readily she did so.

They breakfasted *à deux* (it was Kate's habit never to go to bed before one a.m. and never to face the world before ten) and immediately afterwards set out for the tweed factory.

"Good day to you, sir. How's your father keeping?" It seemed that Douglas could not walk a yard through Carrickdoo without being stopped. Most times the enquirer would add: "And your mother? God help her. We've not seen her since your brother, the Lord have mercy on him, was taken."

Johanna, going into the tiny Post Office to buy stamps, was not unaware of the interest she herself aroused. Everything about her was looked over—her beige-toned lipstick and nail polish, her bib-topped check cotton skirt, her bare legs in the strapped exercise sandals. And when it came to her turn the voice behind the grille was as interested as the eye.

"Lovely day, thank God. Would you be from the hotel?"

"Don't tell her. She's a nosy old bag," Douglas's voice commented from the door, and the postmistress beamed widely in acknowledgement.

"Ah, Mr. O'Malley! Are you together?" The eyes went immediately to Johanna's left hand.

"To put you in the picture, Nora," Douglas said twinkling, "we're fellow guests."

"At the big house with Miss Martin? Sure that's lovely. You're more than welcome." Facts having been established, Nora at last drew forward her battered folder of stamps.

130

O'Malley Tweeds Limited was approached by a short drive with a sign that read encouragingly: "Visitors Welcome." It was a spread of shed type buildings, one with a gabled front, and it had the usual appurtenances of grass plot and flower beds, bicycle racks and loading bay.

The Office Manager, Mr. Grogan, had apparently been expecting them. He rang for coffee to be sent in and invited Mr. Rhatigan, the Works Manager, and Miss McNiely, the Personnel Officer, to join them. Shay, it seemed, had told everyone bout the creator of the new designs and they were all anxious to meet her. It was very flattering and Johanna regretted her bare legs and "little girl" cottons.

"Tell me," Mr. Grogan bade her, "where did they find you at just the psychological moment? Three weeks back Shay was just about doing his nut."

"Saint Anthony sent her," Douglas answered before Johanna could speak. "To me," he added drily, and looked quizzically at her across the little office, his neck broad and suntanned over the roll neck sweater.

For a crazy second it almost seemed as though he meant it, as though they might make a pair in other things than the fact that they were both wearing off-duty clothes—and then the grey eyes looked away and Johanna's pulse returned to normal.

"This money," Douglas said. "I hope they all know to keep quiet about it. It only needs someone to open his mouth in Flaherty's and it'll be all round the place."

Both Mr. Grogan and Mr. Rhatigan looked impressed. "Don't worry about that end of it," the former promised. "They'll all be briefed."

At this point Miss McNiely asked Johanna if she would like "a walk round". They left the room as Douglas was opening a cupboard and glaring at the safe it contained. "I can see what the insurance company is getting at. A clever thief would soon have the back off that."

There was much to see and Miss McNiely was an informative guide. They started with the spinning and dyeing rooms and went on to the department where the weft threads were being wound on to cops to fit the weavers' shuttles. Next came the warping room with its mills taller than a man. A young employee was busy with an immense cocoon-shaped beam which had been disengaged and was being got ready for a weaver. "But it's enormous!" Johanna gasped. Not surprising. The usual length for a piece, she was informed, was seventy yards.

In another part of the factory weaving was actually in progress. The weavers were all young and Miss McNiely explained that they had come to learn the craft. She introduced the elderly man who was supervising and Johanna was struck by his slow courteous way of talking. At the end of the conversation he gave them a grave: "God be with you."

"Now at this stage," Miss McNiely explained, "the beams go out to the weavers. When they come back they go straight to the finishing block." She led Johanna across the yard, talking as they went about the various welfare schemes which had grown with the years. She would have been, Johanna decided, not much younger than Sheila O'Malley and she was obviously dedicated to O'Malley Tweeds.

Listening to her made thoughts of the possible merger more distressing than ever. Not that she supposed it would mean disaster. This nice woman would not lose her job, the shuttles would still clack and the O'Malley vans with their sheep and lamb symbol would still dash through the narrow main street of Carrickdoo. But it would not be a family business any more. There would not be the same sense of pride and personal involvement.

"You look very serious," Miss McNiely commented as they retraced their steps. "Is there anything I've left out that you'd like to see, or . . ."

"Oh no. You've been most kind," Johanna said quickly. "I was just wondering about the O'Malley family." It could make it worse, she warned herself, but for all that she didn't seem able to stop. "The two boys— did you know them when they were children?"

"Indeed I did. Mr. Douglas was about five or six when I first came to work here. I worked for his grandfather in those days. He was still alive."

"About five or six," Johanna repeated. Hard to imagine Douglas as anything but thirty-three, a man's man, complete and sure of himself. "What was he like?"

"Very quiet. Always round his grandfather. He'd an old head on young shoulders even then."

"And Myles?"

"Oh, quite different. Extrovert. Precocious. The white-headed boy." She paused. "I don't know if you heard what really happened, at least why he was going to Scotland the day he was killed."

"No," said Johanna, half-whispering.

Miss McNiely sighed. "Some wretched girl, it seems. Oh, I know that takes two and Mr. Myles would have been more than willing, but I'm old-fashioned, and that sort of thing in a girl makes me see red."

"What—sort of thing?" Johanna demanded sharply.

"You think I'm taking too much for granted. Maybe I am. But if it were all open and above board why make a mystery of it? Anyway, only for her he'd be alive to-day."

Under cover of her deep fringe Johanna could feel beads of perspiration on her brow. "But you don't even know for sure that there was a girl?"

"Not much doubt about it. She rang looking for him the afternoon of the day he was killed. Didn't give her name, but Shay—he was the one answered the phone—said she seemed terribly upset when he told her. I believe Mr. Douglas was thinking at one time of trying to trace her."

"Why?" Johanna could hardly hear her own voice.

"Well, I suppose to bring it home to her." Miss McNiely was a good-looking woman, aquiline-featured and with keen blue eyes. A shade of hardness now crept into them. "Girls to-day—not you, of course, my dear—seem to think they can do anything they please. This one has come near to wrecking a business it's taken years to build. Why shouldn't she know it?"

Strolling through the village again with Flann at heel, he had been waiting at the door of the factory, Douglas remarked humorously: "I *feel* worried, and you *look* it, so what that makes us I'm not quite sure. Sort of a "push-me-pull-u'?" He looked sideways at Johanna. "Perhaps you didn't see 'Dr. Dolittle'?"

She had, and she smiled accordingly. "What are you worried about?"

"This extra money we're holding tonight and to⸗

morrow." He lowered his voice discreetly. The wage claim was nearly six months retrospective and all told something like five thousand pounds would be going out in pay packets on Friday. It entailed a great deal of making up and they had wanted to take it in from the bank on Tuesday, but the insurance company had turned their thumbs down. Can't blame them really. That safe you saw me looking at was put in in my grandfather's time. I could almost take the back off it myself. They've kicked about it already even for our normal requirements and we have a new one on order, but it won't be in for some weeks."

Johanna asked what had been arranged.

"Well, they've given us cover for three thousand and I've held over the balance of the drawing until tomorrow. Tomorrow night we've got to carry the extra two thousand ourselves. And I'm not happy about it. I've got a watchman laid on, but he can't be everywhere and out here in the wilds we don't run to an all-night Garda station." He sighed philosophically. "I think I'll just have to go down and take a turn myself."

At lunch Kate enquired the afternoon's programme and Douglas answered for Johanna. He was taking her down to have tea with Maire O'Malley and was himself going on to see his friend Vincent O'Neill, the vet.

"Don't ring on the front door then, he's given up answering it," Kate warned. "Your only chance is to go straight into the kitchen. I know, I've had to do it. He's got as odd as two left shoes."

"But good heavens, doesn't he still come and look at the zoo for you?"

"No. Never does anything in that line now," she answered sadly.

Johanna, going upstairs to change into her red paisley dress, heard them talking.

"But can't you—I mean," Douglas sounded embarrassed, "surely he'd listen to *you*. A man with his gifts, I doubt if there's a vet to touch him in Ireland. What's the trouble, Kate? What's this research he's on?"

"Supposed to be on," Kate said delicately, and Douglas apparently got the message. "Oh, good *grief*! Not that!" he exclaimed.

Driving Johanna down to the village, however, there was no further talk of Vincent.

Much in Carrickdoo had lived up to the guide books, much had surprised her—the electric typewriters and the dictating machines in the office of O'Malley Tweeds, Kate's little housemaid humming a tune that was number one in the charts, and now Maire O'Malley's home. It should have been a whitewashed cottage, clinging like a barnacle to the hill, with Maire, straight from an Irish song book, dark-haired, blue-eyed and shy. Maire with her mysterious connection with Matthew O'Malley had always been shadowy and petite.

The cottage was out for a start, the bungalow was modern and smart as paint, and Maire O'Malley (it had to be her because Douglas was at that moment hailing her) was tall and striding, brown with crab-apple cheeks and eyes the colour of chestnuts. She had a handful of weeds which she waved unselfconsciously at the car.

"Hallo and welcome!" she was calling in a ringing authoritative voice.

"Lovely to see you, Jo! Shay's told me so much about you." Douglas had gone on his way and Maire O'Malley's brown eyes and wide smile were free to bend themselves warmly on their guest. They had to. Maire was slightly taller than Douglas and a good head over Johanna. Her hair was straight and brown, her long suntanned legs were bare, her lime and lemon dress showed her knees. Shadowy? Shy? Defenceless? Johanna felt like laughing aloud.

The time passed quickly. After tea Johanna was shown over the bungalow. Maire had bought it for a song and was gradually doing it over to her own taste. "Between terms, of course, which doesn't make it any easier."

"Between terms?" Johanna echoed, and learned that Maire had been a teacher before her marriage and as soon as her children were independent had taken a course in Psychology and was now lecturing at a university in the North of England.

And you thought, Johanna reminded herself, a waitress, perhaps, or a chambermaid taken on for the season. "I had no idea. Shay just said you 'did a bit across the water.'"

"Oh, I like the sound of that!" Maire laughed. Of

135

Kate she spoke warmly: "She's an absolute dear, and so played on. They dump all the unwanted animals in the place on her—the ever open door. I tell her she ought to have been Kate Barnardo!"

Only when she was walking back with Johanna to "the big house" did Maire give any hint of what must have been in her mind. "Come and see me again if you've time, and next time you come to Carrickdoo, Shay *must* bring you to stay with me." Her chestnut brown eyes, grave and kind, met Johanna's and could not be lied to.

"I'd like that, Mrs. O'Malley," Johanna said. "But— I don't know."

"Jo dear," the ringing voice had softened, but it still sounded amused, "you really don't have to. The days when you married the first man who brought you home are gone even in Carrickdoo! Gerry Baldwin's been twice or three times."

It was surprising to find that Geraldine had actually stayed in the bungalow. Again she'd drawn a wrong conclusion, she'd thought that Shay had backed a loser from the start.

"You've met Gerry, of course?" Maire was asking. "She's a bright spark. I don't think I've ever laughed so much as the first weekend Shay brought her here. It was supposed to be a work party to paint the bathroom, but the pair of them never stopped fighting. She'd take his hair by the handful and tug it."

"She's going to marry Douglas," Johanna said, and Maire glanced at her.

"So I've heard. Well, he'll keep her in order, none better.

"I like Doug," she continued. "I was always on his side." Johanna started. "Perhaps it's not quite so obvious now that Myles is gone, God rest him." The little phrase not only recalled to Johanna that Maire was a Roman Catholic, it seemed to be literally meant and perhaps it was what Myles, the wild and the charming, had won home to, the peace of God. She came back quickly to what Maire was saying. "But before that, the difference Sheila O'Malley made between those two boys was scandalous. Small wonder Doug chose animals in preference to people."

"I have realised," Johanna offered hesitantly, "that it's not a very happy marriage."

"*Happy?*" Maire echoed. "Oh well, they went into it with their eyes open. Matthew wanted the factory, she wanted a husband to develop it. The one he should have married got left, though he was her friend first, and she's loved him to this day."

Hot-cheeked, Johanna stared. Could this be confirmation of her own suspicions? The reason even for something else unusual—the fact that Shay had been brought up a Protestant. "You mean . . ."

"No names, no pack drill! I've said too much already!" Maire returned. "And Matt's not the worst. For a computer in a jungle of people he's hurt surprisingly few and none of his wounds is fatal." She paused, letting Johanna's mind tick over. Whoever Matthew had ditched all those years ago must have managed to live with it, and no one could deny that this happy-hearted woman had done just that.

"When Jim died," Maire was continuing, "that's my husband. He was Matt's cousin, as like him as peas in a pod, and as unlike as chalk to cheese. When Jim died Matt did far more than I'd any right to expect. I took his help for Shay and the girls and I'm glad now that Shay's paying some of it back. Sheila . . ." She shook her smooth brown head. "No dice! Sheila will never let bygones be bygones. Oh dear!" She caught herself up, looking penitent. "I shouldn't have said that. Forget it."

*Forget it!* Johanna, saying good-bye at Kate's tall open gates, knew that discretion was one thing, forgetfulness quite another.

Douglas rang to say he would not be in to dinner, so Kate arranged for it to be brought to her own sitting-room. "And I think we might have a fire. It gets quite chilly in the evenings."

"Right you are, ma'am," Peg the little maid responded cheerfully. "I'll get a bit of colour from the range."

She returned a moment later with a lighted taper and soon the fire was blazing. Kate's grates might be old-fashioned and expensive to fill, but they looked marvellous in action.

"And what did Maire have to say that's making you

look so serious?" Kate looked quizzically across the table. "My goodness, are you blushing?"

Her eyes met Johanna's, their amusement slowly dying away.

"No," said Johanna confusedly. "It's just the fire. though Mrs. O'Malley did surprise me. I didn't know she was a university lecturer."

"Oh yes, she's a remarkable person," Kate vouchsafed. "You could say unique so far as Carrickdoo is concerned. But that's another story." Was it, Johanna wondered, or one she'd guessed already? "Unique and fulfilled," Kate continued without turning a hair. "As any woman who has borne a son to the man she loves." She looked startled as Johanna's cup rattled against its saucer. "Well, don't you agree? I'd certainly like to have done it."

Johanna felt her eyes widen. "But you—weren't able . . ." she checked.

"Hardly, seeing he went off and married someone else," Kate said calmly. "Let's hope you'll be luckier."

"*Me?*"

"My dear child, that's what Doug brought you here for, isn't it? To ask you to marry him?"

"Oh *no!*" The room seemed to be whirling. "I'm sorry, Miss Martin, you've got it wrong." Johanna pushed her chair back. "*Shay* was bringing me, but had to go to London. Douglas just stepped in. Please don't let him think you—well, *that*—please don't let him think it. He'd be so embarrassed. He was before." She saw Kate's brows knit and rushed on faster. "Because—he's going to marry Geraldine Baldwin. They've got as far as looking at houses."

"Geraldine Baldwin? I've never even heard of her," Kate said, staring. "My dear, I'm sorry." She was now completely serious. "I've embarrassed you. You're going to marry *Shay?*" There was a little pause. "Well, that's it then. We can't all be lucky, I suppose," Kate concluded. "I hoped it was Douglas, I'm so fond of him, but I'll vouch for Shay too. He's straight and sturdy and he'll go far. Best of luck, my dear, I . . ."

"It's not that either," Johanna said, swallowing. "Oh, I know you'll think me crazy. Shay *is* all you say and I'm terribly fond of him and he did ask me to marry

138

him and to come up here and think about it, but . . ." she stopped. It was the first time she'd really seen it crystal clear with no blurred edges and no way round it. "It's no use, I can't."

"Then of course you can't, and stop feeling guilty," Kate advised briskly. "I'm glad we've had this talk," she added. "It's done no harm."

When Douglas returned he was noncommittal about Vincent O'Neill and more interested in persuading Kate and Johanna to go down to O'Flaherty's pub with him for a sing-song. The next night he proposed to be on guard duty and on Friday, he prophesied sagely, there would be a deal too much celebrating of the award to make it healthy.

Flaherty's establishment was nearly as old as Carrick-doo. It had mirrors and dark wood and quite a gathering of customers, all of whom greeted Kate and Douglas with respectful warmth. A touch of the feudal days, Johanna thought, sipping a gin and tonic, but not really on account of "the big house". Most of the men, at a guess, were O'Malley employees. Douglas confirmed that this was so. "For the moment anyway," he added.

"What do you mean?" Kate asked.

He set his glass on the table and seated himself, pulling his chair out of range of passersby. "I'm not sure, but every so often I get the feeling my father's hatching something." He lowered his voice. "We might even be in the market. As I say, I don't know."

"Oh no, Doug!" Kate exclaimed, also in an undertone. "Not now. I don't mind admitting that I thought that was the one consolation about Myles's accident, no more troubles of that kind."

"I don't know," Douglas said again.

To Johanna, looking from one face to another, it did not make sense, at least not the references to Myles. Consolation? Troubles? What could Kate mean? Surely the question of a merger would never have arisen had Myles been alive.

"You may not have known this, Jo," Douglas said abruptly as their eyes met, "but my brother was very anxious to see us made part of a foreign-controlled group. He made several explorations in that direction last year."

"And caused a packet of trouble," Kate commented. "Not that Master Myles ever cared about that. I *will* say it, Doug, it's true."

"I see," Johanna said lamely. Another shock. She'd always taken Myles at his face value, someone utterly dedicated to the family firm.

"But I still don't see why now . . ." Kate ran on. "Matt *is* as well as you say, isn't he?" There was a note of anxiety in her voice.

"Oh yes. Physically he's greatly improved," Douglas said quietly. "I don't know, Kate. I could be quite wrong. He'll tell us when he wants to and not before. So let's leave it at that."

"Would you mind?" Johanna asked suddenly.

He looked at her, now quite serious, his eyes wide and thoughtful.

"Yes," he said simply. "Yes. I would."

Johanna had begun to wonder about the promised sing-song when an old man with a melodeon appeared and sounded a few wheezy notes. A customer set the ball rolling and soon the whole bar was chorussing in joyful, if not always tuneful, unison. All the songs were Irish, some of them well-known, some strange to Johanna's ears but apparently firm favourites.

The singing became quieter and Johanna found her surroundings taking possession of her more and more. The wildness of Ireland, its enchantment and the sense of impermanence held her. Not that Carrickdoo would vanish like the fabled Brigadoon, it would still be there on Sunday, dreaming amongst the hills, but she would be gone. Just a few days of magic, their legacy an ache of love—and loneliness.

She roused herself to hear a voice shout persuasively: "Come on, sir. A bit of an old song!"

Other voices joined in. "Come on, Mr. O'Malley. Somethin' for the wee girl there!" Thunderstruck, she realized that it was Douglas on whom they were calling.

"No good," he was saying, grinning and shaking his head. "Can't sing on a couple of beers. I'm still sober."

On the instant, Liam O'Flaherty, the licensee, poured a large whiskey and set it, amidst cheers, on the table in front of him: "There you are, sir. Compliments of the house."

Douglas looked for a second in rueful amusement and got slowly to his feet. "Right, but remember you've only yourselves to blame."

"He's not really going to sing?" Joanna whispered to Kate in amazement.

"Of course he is. Why not?" Kate whispered back. She did not add that it was a long day since Douglas, old beyond his years and carrying the weight of so much dissension on his broad shoulders, had looked as he did tonight.

Douglas did not show his feelings; neither at seven when his mother, coming in from the factory and finding him hovering hopefully in the hall, would say: "Oh dear! Aren't you in bed yet? What's Nancy doing?" nor at twelve or thirteen when the cry was: "Och, Douglas! Give that to wee Myles, please. Can't you see he wants it?" And hardly at all through the battle that had raged over his becoming a vet. No highflown speeches, just a dogged determination that had earned him: "I don't know where we got Douglas from, he couldn't be less like Myles."

Douglas had quite a good voice, though it was always Myles's voice that had been heard on village platforms. Douglas sang only when bludgeoned into it. Or when, perhaps, it was a way of saying something his lips could not.

He had chosen a song of Donegal. "She Moved Through The Fair."

*"My young love said to me: 'My mother won't mind."*

Johanna had heard it better sung, but never quite like this. A light over Douglas's head gave a sort of shine to his eyes. She thought it must have been the light that kept him from altering his position. He had hardly moved a muscle and he was staring straight at her.

*"She moved through the fair*
*And fondly I watched her move here and move there."*

Almost as though . . . but no, she mustn't think it . . . it was absurd, ludicrous, wrong. And yet there *had* been moments when he'd watched her, so kindly, so gently, moments like that night on the hill when she'd felt homesick and he'd pointed out the lights of the airport, moments like that night when he'd sat on the floor and watched her brushing her hair, moments like yesterday by the Fairy Bridges when he'd had good reason to watch, in case she'd fall over. Yes, that was all, sense and kindness, good reason. . . .

*"It will not be long, love, till our wedding day."*

Just as long as never, Johanna thought, just as long as never.

Fine thing, you making such an ass of yourself over another chap's girl, Douglas thought, and sang the last note.

## CHAPTER THIRTEEN

" 'TIS A lot better now, o' course," Paddy, Kate's general factotum, declared next morning as Douglas and Johanna were setting out for the hills. "There's a good steam-rollered road now, so there is."

Douglas was taking her to see Brendan O'Connor, Shay's grandfather. Brendan's cottage was twenty miles from Carrickdoo.

Douglas was an almost silent companion, and Johanna kept remembering unhappily that he had waited an hour after breakfast to see if Kate would like to come with them. That could only mean that he had not wanted to be alone with her. Last night she had . . . oh, don't think of it, she commanded herself, poppy-cheeked, as the car drew up.

Brendan's cottage, low, whitewashed and thatched, with a tiny porched door, stood, like Carrickdoo itself, in a fertile dip. A fine rowan tree grew close by and there was plenty of green undergrowth. Ahead, behind, and on each side, the tops of mountains, blue and misty mauve, stood out against the sky like knuckles and like foreheads and like old men's chins.

142

Brendan O'Connor had a chin like that, clean-cut and pointed with age. He came up the boreen before they had time to knock and he was leading a donkey which was carrying across its shoulders twin baskets of turf.

Proudly he showed her the loom which had been in his family for generations and demonstrated it, gravely and pedantically. A master craftsman, he viewed with suspicion the chemical dyes now in use and spoke nostalgically of the vegetable dyes and the shades produced by the lichens gathered off the high boulders of Errigal, Donegal's highest mountain. Those stormy browns, brown-reds and yellows were, he vowed, the traditional Donegal colours, just as in Connemara the chief dyes were reds and purples from the fuchsias.

"But nowadays 'tis all changed, o'course," he said disgruntledly.

"And a good thing," Douglas put in unexpectedly. "Fair's fair, Brendan. There's a lot more in the stocking now than there used to be—for everyone."

"Have you a story for Miss Dykes?" he asked in a more conciliatory tone. "She's come an awfully long way to hear one."

"Is that right?" Old Brendan looked considerably mollified. "Well, I suppose it'ud never do to disappoint her."

With obvious pleasure he launched into the tale of Brendan the Navigator, his patron saint, it seemed, who in the twelfth century had set sail in a currach from his home in Kerry to find the mythical Isles of the Blest, and, if his latter day namesake were to be believed, had succeeded in finding instead just about every other piece on the globe.

"I don't know what Columbus thought *he* was doing," Johanna whispered to Douglas as Shay's grandfather described how the saint found Newfoundland, the Bahamas and Florida.

"Ah, sure, God help him, he wasn't a Kerryman," came the reply. It seemed like a welcome break through but, driving back to Carrickdoo, Douglas was again taciturn.

"Thank you for taking me. It was wonderful," Johanna ventured.

"Pleasure," he responded briefly. "Shay thinks the world of Brendan. He was most anxious you should meet him. And by the way," his tone was distant, "if you want to see Maire again feel quite free. I'll have to be at the factory this afternoon and tomorrow. I don't know what Kate is planning."

Kate, it turned out at lunch, was planning to take Johanna into the neighbouring town which was having a festival. She had obviously taken it for granted that Douglas would accompany them. He, however, excused himself with a quick downward glance, Johanna watching, made the poignant discovery that Douglas embarrassed was dearer than ever. He looked just a lump of a lad as he sat there with the flush rising in his cheekbones. He wasn't busy, she was sure of it, he just wanted to spend as little time as possible with her. Last night, when he was singing, he must have seen her looking at him and been afraid that other people would see it too.

He *hadn't* been looking at her. How could she have thought it? A trick of the light, that was all, and now he was wishing, as he must often have wished before, that he had never set eyes on her.

The festival, which in other circumstances would have been wholly delightful, managed, however, to salvage some of the afternoon.

On the homeward run Kate pulled up suddenly, pointing to a car parked by the roadside, long, wide, green and with a Dublin registration. Twenty-five yards away was a tinkers' encampment and in it, amongst a crowd of children, a figure in a greenish tweed jacket. The figure, which on its own admission should have been busy at the factory, appeared to be handing out sweets. Kate's finger was on the horn when Johanna stopped her.

"No, please, if you don't mind. He . . ."

Kate could have argued. She didn't. She had left the engine running and now her foot went to the accelerator. If Douglas saw them it was as a passing car.

"And now," Kate demanded crisply, "what *is* all this? What's happened between you and Doug? Oh, but there is!" she retorted as Johanna began to shake her head. "I sat between the two of you at lunch. I'm not blind."

144

"He's my employer and Shay's friend. There's nothing else between us *to* happen," Johanna said desperately.

"Except for you both to admit that you've fallen in love," Kate remarked calmly. "Why not, my dear? What's so distasteful about it?"

"Distasteful?" Johanna stammered. "It's not distasteful. It's impossible. There's Shay, there's Geraldine Baldwin . . ."

"I'll believe she exists when I see her," Kate murmured obstinately. "And Shay's no dog in the manger."

"You've missed the point, Miss Martin," Johanna said edgily. "Douglas doesn't love me."

"No? My dear, if you were a betting woman I could have the shirt off your back. I knew Douglas was in love with you the moment he coaxed me into giving him Amber."

"Coaxed you?" Johanna stared. "But I thought you were looking for a home for him."

Suddenly a vision of Ken rose before her, the exquisiteness of the rose-pink mouth against amber fur and stiff frost-white whiskers, the plumy cream-barred tail, the brassy glaze of gold along the spine. "I should have known," she said humbly. "Shouldn't I?"

"Oh, my darling, I'm only too glad, specially now that I've met you," Kate acknowledged. "Won't you help him out, Jo? If he doesn't know yet that you're not going to marry Shay, tell him."

And so they got married and lived happily ever after, Johanna thought. It was a gross over-simplification. No matter what Kate might choose to believe there was still Geraldine, and she herself was the girl whose whereabouts Douglas in a fit of cold grief had once thought of tracing. She shuddered. "Miss Martin . . ."

"Kate."

"Kate, then," Johanna smiled, and went on more softly, "You're asking me to throw myself at a man who doesn't want me. Would *you* do it?"

The pause was sharp. "I'd let him know," said Kate slowly. "And then, if I had to, I'd face it."

"With . . ." Johanna paused and went on again. The flash of insight was too strong to be stifled even by delicacy. "With animals instead of people?"

"I suppose it happened that way, it wasn't planned." The car slowed at a road junction. "But yes, I have thought it, and that I didn't want—*his son*—to do it too.

"I'm Douglas's godmother," Kate said to Johanna's wondering eyes. "I did think once that I might have been his mother."

It was becoming clear, the man who'd gone away "and married someone else", and the girl who, in Maire's more direct phrasing, "he should have married."

"Thirty-five years ago, Mary McNiely, Sheila Mac-Sweeney, myself or any one of the girls in Carrickdoo would have given their eyes for Matt. I'd a head start because he used to stay at our house, but I would have made him a poor wife and he knew it."

"Maire O'Malley says he married for the factory," Johanna began indignantly.

"He set a price on himself, yes," Kate agreed. "With his brain and his looks he could afford to. He came from Galway, and as you probably know the Spanish Armada was wrecked along the west coast of Ireland and there are people living there to-day with Spanish blood in their veins. The O'Malleys all had it, but Matthew was the cream."

"And Mrs. O'Malley—Douglas's mother—was impervious to all that?" Johanna questioned. "Maire told me it was a marriage of convenience on both sides."

"Yes, Maire would say that," Kate returned, letting the car almost trundle through the narrow main street of Carrickdoo. "She's a good friend of mine and she likes to show the flag! But she's prejudiced. Thirty-four years ago, Matt made a deliberate choice and the tweed factory was only part of it. My father's money would have bought him a business anywhere he liked and he knew it. The choice was between two people, Sheila and me. He liked me, I think, we always had fun together and I wasn't bad looking, but apart from that—" she shook her head comically, "very lightweight. Sheila was quite different. A gawky eighteen-year-old, she never did a thing with herself till Matt took her in hand, but the potential was there. She'd been running the house since her mother died and she'd been into the factory workings with her father and she knew exactly how many beans made five. There

146

was no question really which of us was the better value."

"There is a little bit more to marriage than house-keeping and business methods," Johanna submitted.

"People are different," Kate answered. "To me, yes. I put my eye on Matthew thirty-five years ago and no one else would do. So here I am, and it would be no harm if Sheila took a good hard look at me now and again. Nothing can bring Myles back, and if she won't fill the gap with what Shay can give she stands a very good chance of losing the lot. Impervious to Matthew, did you say? She was crazy about him, all she ever wanted was for him to be crazy about her. If she could have accepted that Matt isn't the romantic kind she'd have saved herself thirty-four years of insecurity and bitterness. Why do you think Doug had such a thin time as a child? Simply and solely because he didn't take after the O'Malleys. In looks and everything else he could have been old John MacSweeney. But Sheila wanted sons like Matthew, nothing else would do. I'm talking a lot, child, it's because I want you to know what Douglas has been up against."

"And I'm very grateful," Johanna said softly. "I suppose it's been easier for—Maire—to believe that there was nothing there anyway. Nothing, I mean, that might have been saved if she'd acted differently."

There was a pause, this time a long one. Kate, now approaching her own gates, let one hand slip to her knee and turned for a second.

"I think you'd better tell me what you do mean, Jo, so I can put you right." There was withdrawal in the tone.

Johanna swallowed. "I've tried not to think it, Kate, but so many people have hinted or have seemed to hint that Shay—is Douglas's and Myles's half-brother. Even you yourself, I thought, when you said Maire was unique in Carrickdoo and that she'd borne a son to the man she loved."

"Good heavens, child!" Kate was staring at her. "*You didn't let her guess?* She'd be cut to the quick. She did bear a son to the man she loved, he was her husband. When I said she was unique . . ." She broke off for a moment. "Did I put the idea into your head or did you come with it there already?"

"I did." Uncomfortably Johanna related Matthew's

apparent embarrassment when she'd made her first mistake about Shay's relationship to Douglas, his concerned question that night when he'd thought Maire was ill, and even, though now she was intensely ashamed of them, Alice's insinuations.

Not a muscle of Kate's face moved as she listened. "You've taken my breath away," she said at the close. "I had no idea of this. It could even be that Sheila . . ." She did not finish. Brisking up as the house, with the usual feline guard on the gravel, came into view, she concluded: "Maire is unique because she didn't lose one night's sleep over Matt. He *was* attracted to her. Jim O'Malley introduced them just before the wedding and it was quite something to see Matt smitten for once. But it came to nothing. Maire saw to that. As a matter of fact I think Sheila owed Myles to her. Matt needed a woman just then. It seemed like a fresh start, but it wasn't, and only now do I begin to understand why." She switched off the engine. "Jo, the irony of it! Even Shay's religion helped, I suppose. You see it was a mixed marriage, and as you know it's almost unheard of for the children not to be Catholics, but—that's another reason why I said she was unique—Maire was absolutely determined that young Shay should belong to his father's Church. I don't necessarily defend her, but that was how she saw it and that was that."

"Will you say anything?" Johanna faltered, opening her door.

"I don't think so. What good would it do? I know Shay is Jim's son, but if it comes to it what proof could I offer? This is something Sheila will have to accept and live with, even if she's never a hundred per cent sure. That's life, Jo, isn't it? Trusting people."

At dinner Kate took the bull by the horns. "We saw you!" she told Douglas. "At the tinker camp."

"Oh yes?" he returned off-handedly. "I was having a nose round, as a matter of fact. Not much goes on in the townland that those chaps don't know about."

"And did they?" Kate pressed.

"You can depend on it they do," Douglas said. "But they're not for talking." He changed the subject in favour of the regatta.

Johanna had gone upstairs for a cardigan. She did not hurry down and when she reached the hall again Kate and Douglas were there. Kate, looking excited, explained that there had been a phone call from a friend who was expecting her first baby.

"I think I'll go over," she concluded. "It may be a false alarm, but her husband's away till tomorrow and she sounded uneasy. If it is the baby I'll have to stay with her." She glanced at Johanna. "You won't mind, will you, dear? I know Doug's going to be out, but Cook and Peg and Paddy will all be here."

Some minutes later Douglas observed casually, "It's a nice evening. I was wondering would you like to come for a run?"

"Yes, but aren't you going to the factory?" Johanna asked amazedly.

"That can wait for a bit. Nothing will happen in daylight."

"I thought we might go to the shore," he said as they got into the car. "Sit!" he added sternly to Flann on the back seat.

It was like coming home, though home must have been nearly six hundred miles away and there were no airport lights to wink a message of comfort. There was just a hefty shoulder in green Harris tweed and on the wheel the hands that had hauled her up Aughrus Head.

"It's the blue hour," she said delightedly as the car came to a stop.

Douglas turned to her with a listening air. It was something she'd always noticed about him, he didn't interrupt. His eyes had the blue glint she loved and for "keeping eyes" they were very clear. For a giddy moment she saw them as "family" eyes twinkling at some very small V.I.P., snapping shut as a tiny starlike palm went up to the network of wrinkles at their corners. Bemusing thoughts followed, Douglas giving that rare smile to a baby daughter, Douglas walking along with a pocket edition of himself instead of always just Flann.

"You'll be glad to get home," Douglas said abruptly. "You must feel very lonely here at times."

"Lonely?" Off-guard, she did not think of discretion. "Here—with you? Oh no." Recollection flooded her.

She said awkwardly, "I'm sorry, that was a very silly thing to say, but nobody heard."

"*I* did, I'm thankful to say," Douglas remarked. "I didn't find it at all silly and I should be quite glad for the whole world to hear. It made me feel ten feet tall." He took the hand he was holding and parcelled it in both his. "I should be telling you what a great job you've done, but all I can think of is how much I'll hate saying good-bye to you."

It was a dizzy moment. She didn't know, as they said, whether she was coming or going. It didn't make sense, it *mustn't* make sense, but Douglas's eyes had all that dark shining look they'd had in O'Flaherty's establishment and somehow even his hands seemed to be talking.

"Me too," she gasped. "I've enjoyed it all so much, specially up here."

"Specially the last hour," Douglas said calmly. "After Kate told me you weren't going to marry Shay."

"She had only just time for a quick word," he added. "Because you were coming down the stairs, but she told me that, and she said I should ask what made you think I didn't want that sort of thing. So I'm asking—because the truth is it would be my wish come true."

Johanna wondered if he could hear her heart. It seemed to be making the whole world vibrate. This could not happen, she could not let it happen, and yet it seemed that for the moment anyway she could no more stop it than she could stop the waves hissing into palest ice-blue foam against the rocks.

"Oh, Doug," she whispered, "I don't know what to say."

But even for this there seemed to be an answer. The green jacket was spread on one of the rocks and Douglas pulled her gently down to sit on it. She felt, still dizzily, that it was like being enthroned.

"You won't take cold with this." He swept her unconcernedly into the circle of a vast arm. "Not for a few minutes anyway. What did I say, my lamb, what damn fool thing did I do to make you think I didn't want you?"

When she told him about his mother's warning and the construction she had put upon it he still looked helpless. "I'm afraid I'm none the wiser, love, but it was certainly not I. If I had to, I'd do my own choking off."

"I didn't have to, though," he appended with mock pathos. "You never did it again."

It seemed a good enough invitation for any girl. Johanna's hand went up and drew the fine head and the big boyish lips down to hers.

"Well?" Douglas asked tenderly. "Do I bring a designer into the family? You realize, of course, it's the only reason I'm proposing?"

"Proposing?" Johanna's head jerked. "You mean— you're asking me to m-marry you?"

"Not asking—insisting," said Douglas.

She thought frantically. Where was her backbone? It was weak to start thinking: "Shay won't tell. He promised. And I could warn Mum and Dad. There's no other possible loophole." For the odd few seconds that seemed eternity indecision swung before her like a pendulum. "Oh, I can't, I *mustn't*." And back again: "I must think. Is there *no* way round it?"

"Please let me think about it," she began, and put her hand to his forehead as it creased. "Not because I don't love you. I do. Just that I never thought, quite honestly, I never thought until this minute that *you* loved *me*. And I want to think about that, tonight, on my own, just for a few hours before I say anything. It's a sort of girl thing," she ended doubtfully. "You mightn't understand."

Douglas was surveying her seriously.

"You know, for a girl thing, that's got quite a complimentary ring somewhere." He smiled so that the lines round his eyes crinkled. "All right. Just so long as it's 'yes' tomorrow, it'll give *me* something to think about tonight too." He put his cheek to hers and they sat for a few minutes close together and silent.

"Are you really expecting trouble?" Johanna asked anxiously as Douglas, having brought her back to "the big house", turned to set out on his vigil.

"No, not really," he answered, truthfully, she felt. "But I've said I'll be there, so I must."

He walked sturdily to the car where Flann was waiting. The dog had taken advantage of Johanna's departure to scramble into the front seat and he gave his master's forehead a lick of welcome. It was almost as though he were saying: "She not coming? Good." Johanna had to admit that she had not really made such headway with Flann. He was supremely a one-person dog. Now, as the car went down the drive, the two heads were level and side by side.

Kate rang to say she was still with her friend and might have to take her to the hospital. Johanna said goodnight to Peg who was in the hall and went upstairs. Sleep was out of the question. She sat by the window, thinking desperately. What had seemed a clearcut "Yes" or "No" became with each moment more complex.

She had thought the age of miracles was over, but one had just happened. *Douglas loved her.* And with every fibre of her being she loved him. Could she marry him with the past unconfessed, never knowing the moment when she might betray herself? On the other hand, could she tell him?

Bit by bit the nuances of the problem emerged. Douglas at this moment might well opt for love, but afterwards there would always be that little canker in the bud . . . "It wasn't her fault, but—only for Johanna Myles would still be alive and my father would not have sold out." And besides, Douglas was a man of his word. Now that he had proposed to her he would go through with it no matter what. *Tell him at this stage and she would never know how he really felt.*

So telling him was impossible, but giving him up equally so. She would say "yes" and keep the past to herself. After all, as the old rhyme put it, seven magpies stood for a secret which should never be told.

It was after one when she went to bed and then she slept brokenly, waking once to an odd sound like water cascading somewhere quite far away. It seemed that she had just turned over when she woke again.

"What is it? What's after happening?" Cook's voice was shouting. There was an answer, inaudible to Johanna's ears, and a further exclamation: "I knew it! I toldt ye! And herself not here!"

"What's up?" Peg's softer tones could now be heard. "What's all the row?"

Three voices replied, Cook's overriding the others. "Them dirty tinkers! Mr. Douglas is after getting hurted!"

Johanna, falling out of bed, caught her toe in the sheet, kicked free and thrust her head wildly through a window. It was light enough to see Cook's head protruding from another and Peg's from a third. Paddy was outside on the gravel, and with him another young man.

"Paddy, what's happened?" Johanna shouted.

He looked up. A slow-witted youth, she could almost see the thoughts going through his head. "Bit of trouble below at the factory. Not much at all, though. Don't be worryin' your head."

He said this half a dozen times as most reluctantly he took Johanna down to the factory. The other youth who lived in the village and had been roused by the excitement accompanied them. Douglas had left his car in the road-way some distance from the factory. It was still there and as they passed it in the half light, its windows all closed, it had a ghostly air.

"Where is Mr. O'Malley?" Johanna asked sharply. "And where's his dog?"

Paddy's friend ignored the reference to Flann. Douglas, he said, had gone to the hospital to have his head looked at. "Hospital?" Johanna's blood began to run cold. "But you never said . . ."

They had said only that there had been an attempted robbery. Now she drew out the details. It had been timed to coincide with a fire at the tinkers' camp which had engaged the attention of the police. The sound Johanna had heard had been not water but the distant crackling of flames. Two tents had been destroyed, but nobody had been injured. Meantime, at the factory, the two raiders, expecting a clear field, had walked straight into Douglas's arms. In the ensuing struggle he had accounted for one of them and that one was now in custody. The second man, however, had seemingly struck Douglas on the head and made his getaway. The safe remained intact and the police were reasonably hopeful of picking up the villain still at large.

"And Mr. O'Malley will be all right?" Johanna asked the C.I.D. sergeant.

"Too early to say, miss," was the far from encouraging reply. Douglas had been taken unconscious to the County Infirmary.

"Nothing you can do here, miss," Paddy said, well-meaning as ever. "Come on, I'll take you back.' He seemed anxious to get her away. Why anxious? she thought dully in the middle of a prayer. She'd been praying like a prayer wheel; fast as she finished, starting it again. . . . "Please, God, take care of him, make him better. . . ."

"That's right, miss. You go home and ring the hospital. They'll tell you how he is." Realization of what she was looking for came as the sergeant spoke. *What* she was looking for . . . it was *who*. "Flann. Where's Flann got to, Paddy? *Where's Flann?*"

No one told her. There was no need to. She read it in Paddy's shifting eyes and the swift light anger in the sergeant's.

"It was quick like," Paddy said awkwardly. "He couldn't a' suffered."

Flann had been found beside his master. Someone had used a knife on him. The sergeant said it was the kind of thing that made him see red. He was fond of dogs and "that one was a beauty". He handed Paddy the keys of Douglas's car and told him to take Johanna home in it.

None of it could truthfully be termed callous. For the crime squad the world was not threatening to come to an end and there was still much to do. It was just brisk and final. A nightmare. Only let her get away, Johanna thought, and she might wake up. She was halfway to the car when she stopped.

"What about Flann?"

"Can't do no more for him, miss," Paddy said with truth. "The Guards will see to it."

"No," she said sharply. "We can't leave him."

Paddy was horrified. "No, miss. It'ud turn you, so it would."

She couldn't hope to explain the feeling that she was now part of Douglas, the part of him that could still act, and that this was something she must do or never live with herself again. She turned wordlessly and ran to the factory door.

There was blood—she tried not to think about it. It had stained the white flash on Flann's chest and his one white toe. His head, however, from occiput to nose, was unmarred and noble. Johanna kneeled and stroked it. What had happened in those few moments only Douglas and his assailant could tell, but there seemed little doubt that Flann, "the man of peace", had given his life for his master.

She ran her hand from the foreface down to the neck. Somehow, it was all so much less alien than she'd expected. Surely by now, some sort of change . . . she frowned and touched the chest. A tremor, faint but unmistakable, passed through the inert form. "Paddy!" Johanna yelled. "I don't think he's dead!"

Only Paddy, however, shared her belief that it was a miracle. The Guards shook their heads. "He's beyond aid, miss," and she read their thoughts.

"No, please. You mustn't. Not yet. Paddy, don't let them!"

Kindly the sergeant pointed out that there was now no veterinary surgeon in Carrickdoo, the nearest was twelve miles away and it was unfair to rouse him at four o'clock in the morning for a dog who was mortally injured.

"I'll take him to Mr. O'Neill," Johanna said impulsively.

The Guards looked at each other. The sergeant cleared his throat:

"You'd be wasting your time, Miss Dykes. You won't find him sober."

Bit by bit, the sense of miracle was ebbing. Flann was living, but only just. Twice she had thought he'd stopped breathing. And could she really see herself bearing Vincent O'Neill? Terror crept into her toes and spread coldly. She looked down white-faced at the blood. And then for the second time she was pulling herself together, saying to the sergeant: "It's all I can do," and to Paddy: "Bring the car down. Quickly! He's still alive."

After that, extraordinarily, she ceased to feel afraid. She was there in the thick of it and fighting. Every jolt, every minute had to be reckoned with. So had loss of blood. There was still that odd sensation of not being herself as she crouched over Flann, shielding him when the car bumped, using her fingers to close the widest wound.

Paddy braked in a dark drive. She slipped away from her patient and knocked on Vincent O'Neill's front door. Kate had warned that these days he did not answer it and though the sound woke echoes in the sleeping house there was no sign of response. It still seemed that the various parts of her acted without recourse to her normal timid self. Her feet took her to the back door, her hand tried its handle and found it unlocked, her voice shrill with emotion called from the foot of the stairs.

"Mr. O'Neill! Excuse me. Are you there?"

It was again her limbs that took over, opening one of the downstairs doors, switching on the light and sending her with a gasp across the room to the man asleep in a chair, a big man with rosy cheeks and a shock of thick white hair.

"Mr. O'Neill!"

He slumbered on, his chin sunk in the heavy roll of brown Aran sweater.

"Mr. O'Neill—I'm sorry," she babbled. "I've a dog outside."

The eyes opened, tired, blue and angry. "What the . . ."

"He's nearly dead. He's been knifed." She watched as

the blue eyes started to close. "Mr. O'Neill!" Again it was not her. Something outside her sent her hands desperately to the broad shoulders, gripping them and shaking. "Wake up! It's Flann—Douglas O'Malley's dog. *Douglas O'Malley!*"

"What happened?" Vincent O'Neill was heaving himself to his feet. She told him as they went out to the car. "Who have you got with you?" he asked, smoothing his hair with both hands.

"Just Paddy Malone." She had heard Kate say Paddy was employed for heart and not intellect and after tonight she knew exactly what that meant. "But he's been wonderful and I'll do anything you tell me."

They had reached the car and the veterinary surgeon was looking with pursed lips at his patient. "You'll have to do more than that," he said drily. "You'll have to do the impossible. So will I."

The following hour in the small disused surgery made it plain that Vincent O'Neill was no stranger to the impossible. His fingers worked with tireless precision. He stopped only once to go to the sink and sluice cold water over his face. Johanna worked too, like an automaton, passing instruments, holding Flann steady, swabbing, doing anything she was asked. She still felt disorientated and as though at any moment the curtain would come down and fatigue overpower her.

At last Vincent O'Neill straightened wearily and she knew that for good or ill it was over.

"Right. Here's where we let nature take over. You did well," he told Johanna. "So did I." She felt it said a lot.

Kate, on the telephone some time later, said a good deal more. The Guards had located her and she had gone straight to the county hospital where she would wait until Sheila O'Malley arrived. There had been no change in Douglas's condition, but he was holding his own.

"Wait till he hears about Flann," Kate said joyously. "Oh, darling, I don't know which of you is the more wonderful, you or Vincent."

"Kate," Johanna quavered. The curtain had come down at last blotting out everything but the fears she'd held at bay. "*Will* he hear?"

Despite Kate's assurances, prolonged and extra-firm, the next twelve hours were grim. Johanna, wanting to follow in to the hospital, found herself under orders to stay at home and rest. Rest! How could you rest when any minute the phone might ring and Kate say: "I'm sorry, darling. They did all they could." Unable to sit still, she fretted the moments away in movements that led nowhere, up Kate's front stairs, through the rambling corridors and down the back stairs again to the kitchen.

The afternoon brought Maire O'Malley full of praise for the Flann episode which it seemed was being widely discussed, and shortly before her arrival Vincent O'Neill telephoned a most encouraging progress report.

"You realize how wonderful it is—and not just for the dog." Maire's eyes looked warmly into Johanna's. "I take off my hat to you, Jo. This could be a break-through."

The awful thing was that Johanna knew all this and now hardly cared. Douglas was still unconscious. Kate's last communication, as always resolutely cheerful, had hinted that he might be moved to a hospital in Dublin which specialized in head injuries.

"Kate doesn't want to worry me, but I *know*," she said tremulously. "He's very ill."

"Yes, love," Maire agreed, "he is. But he's also as strong as an ox and he's got everything to live for." She gave Johanna a look of searching tenderness. "You love him, don't you?"

"It happened. I didn't mean it to." This was all wrong. Shay deserved at least the first admission. "Shay's been so good to me. I thought . . . I'm so fond of him "

"Don't worry about Shay," Maire said firmly. "I understand. He will too."

She stayed on, coaxing Johanna to have first tea and then a little dinner. They were still at the table when car wheels crunched on the drive. A pale-faced Kate came up the steps looking as though she could barely lift her feet. Johanna flew out to meet her and she opened her arms to her.

"Better news, darling, quite a bit better." Sheila had arrived some hours ago, Matthew with her. "You know how stiff he gets after a drive," Kate said compassionately. "This was such a long one he could hardly stand." Douglas had come round and had seemed to know his parents before he had again lost consciousness.

"The shock probably did that," Maire commented forthrightly. "Can you imagine, Kate, when he last saw those two beside his bed? Even when he was a baby it's doubtful if Matt took time off to notice him."

"You're too hard on Matt," Kate said loyally. "He had a business to build, remember. And anyway, something's happened to him. He's changed." From her tone it did not seem that she was happy about the change.

The hospital's next bulletin continued to be restrainedly optimistic and the morning one was much better. Douglas had had a comfortable night and was fully conscious. This caused Kate to telephone Sheila at the hotel near the hospital where she and Matthew had put up and insist that they transfer to Carrickdoo and stay with her.

"It's not easy for Matthew in a hotel," she told Johanna.

Thirty-five years, Johanna thought, and she still loves him. It could nearly have been her own love for Douglas, condemned to live on only as a memory.

> *"And when I lost my heart so willingly so many years ago*
> *I lost it, love, to you."*

It took a lot of heart to lose and still live as cheerfully as Kate.

# CHAPTER FOURTEEN

THE white Mercedes brought Sheila and Matthew from the hospital. For Kate, who had not played host to Matthew since he had become markedly disabled, it was an emotional occasion.

He looked all in and there were puffy marks like bruises under his eyes. Johanna was not surprised when Sheila reappeared alone and said she had persuaded him to rest till dinner. Sheila, however, did surprise her. Town clothes had been replaced by slacks and a proofed jacket and she invited Johanna to go for a walk with her.

They made their way along the shore road. Sheila had a long stride and she walked with her hands in her pockets like a boy. The wind whipped her short copper hair and she looked a world removed from the soignée figure known to O'Malley House. And perhaps, Johanna thought, a world nearer to the "gawky eighteen-year-old" who had been John MacSweeney's only child.

As they walked, she continued to talk freely both of the encouragingly long visit they had been allowed to pay Douglas that morning and the excellent news Shay had given them from London. Mr. Felgate-Winter had not only signed up Young O'Malley for himself, he had put Shay in touch with an interested French firm, so instead of returning to Dublin, Shay and Geraldine were going on to Paris on Monday. "I do feel we owe a lot of that to you, Jo. Your designs were so good. I hope Carrickdoo has given you lots more ideas."

It had, its rock patterns, its sea blues, its landscape touches of brassy gold. Johanna wished she had had longer time to absorb it.

"But of course you're not going on Monday now," Sheila insisted. "Douglas will be ready for visitors after the weekend and I know he wants to thank you for saving

Flann." For a second she looked away. "It was such a shock. He's never been ill in his life. I'd got used to . . ." she checked. "Jo, I want you to tell me something. Kate says Doug thought my husband was making changes in the business. Did he by any chance talk to you about them?"

"Me?" Johanna managed a gasp of astonishment. "Why should Mr. O'Malley talk to me?"

"Because he likes you," Sheila said simply. "Make no mistake about that. You wouldn't have lasted a week at home if he hadn't. Believe me, I speak from experience." The brown eyes which could be sharp and teasing and sometimes off-putting were now only warm. "I've often thought, you know, that you and Myles would have made the perfect pair."

Four or five weeks in Ireland should have blunted the edge of such remarks, but they hadn't. There was still that whirling breath-catching sensation. Johanna felt desperately that there always would be.

"And very happy I would have been about it," Sheila added disarmingly. "Meantime, there's still my question. I'll get nothing out of Matt till he chooses. I can't worry Doug at the moment. And I haven't got Myles on my side any more."

"On your side!" The words were out before Johanna could contain them. "But Myles wanted . . ." Aghast, she stopped.

"Go on," Sheila prompted drily. "Go *on*, Jo. Don't you think it's time I heard?"

So many hands, so many strings and all pulling against each other. To Johanna, it was little short of tragedy. Sheila, Matthew, Douglas, all wanted the same thing— the continuation of O'Malley Tweeds Ltd.

"Yes, Mrs. O'Malley," she said steadily, "I think it is."

In the bedroom Matthew had set about changing for dinner. Nothing in his whole day made him more irritable than dressing and undressing. He could not pull his shirt over his head. He dropped things and could not pick them up. At this moment, the tie he had chosen, an embossed shot silk, lay on the floor.

"Pick up that thing, will you?" he said resentfully as Sheila entered.

It was another thing she had taken for granted, the services Douglas had performed as a matter of routine for his father. The phone to his flat must sometimes have rung twenty times a day with the curt request to "come here, will you?" Never me, she thought, unless both Douglas and Shay were unavailable. If it had not been for the factory he would have got out long ago.

Mechanically now, she took out his fresh shirt, a heavy cream silk. Matthew on his deathbed, like as not, would be fussing over his shirts.

"I'll have to learn this, won't I?" she said, easing the lustrous folds over his darkly tanned arms.

"What for?"

Help me, she prayed silently.

"Well, I've been thinking, Matt, you and I should meet Felgate-Winter—and the French crowd. Give Young O'Malley top promotion."

His face, almost vacant with surprise, stared back.

"Of course we'd have to sound Dr. Hunter," she said delicately. "But he can only say no."

"So we give him the chance to, do we?" Matthew looked vacant no longer. He was bright, dark, and in spate again. "That's the thing I'm up against every day— passing the buck, defeatism. What's it to Hunter? I'm the one has to keep things on the move. Well . . ." he broke off, "fifty per cent of it, I suppose."

"Thank you, Matthew," Sheila said sweetly.

He caught the smile and the big-eyed oblique glance She saw him flush and look away. But he looked back. "Have I walked into something?"

"That, Matt, is entirely up to you." She had been unbuttoning her jacket and she let it fall on to her bed. "You make the decisions, remember?"

Except for last night's uncomfortable few hours in the hotel, it was years since she and Matthew had shared a bedroom, years since she'd hurried gauchely into the trousseau Carrickdoo's dressmaker had turned out, years since Matthew had looked at her and doubled up in laughter. Cruel laughter, she'd thought, hurt to the quick. Thirty-four years later it had been, she realized, very funny. Now, she washed quite unhurriedly and selected a slip, cream-coloured, its top a froth of deep lace.

"What have I walked into?" Matthew asked. "Oh, confound it!" He had dropped the handkerchief he was folding. "No, let me get it myself." He leaned forward precariously. "I'm not out on grass yet." The dark eyes flickered strangely. She'd had thirty-five years to get used to them, but suddenly she looked away, picked up her dress, and eased it quickly over her head.

"Then Doug was wrong?" she shot it at him.

"Doug? Wrong? What about?" He had not succeeded in retrieving the handkerchief. It still lay on Kate's cherry carpet.

"Oh, Matt!" They could go on fencing like this for hours. "You know exactly what I mean. This merger. Doug got wind of it." Better to keep Jo out of it. The child had spoken under protest and only after an inward struggle. She'd seen that. "He told Kate."

"History repeating itself?" Matthew muttered.

"All right." She would let him have it now. She was raw and tired. "He always loved Kate, he hasn't changed. She always loved you, Matt, and she hasn't changed either. You always . . ." she checked. There was no point in two middle-aged people behaving like children.

"Don't stop now," Matthew said calmly. "For Pete's sake, Sheila, after thirty-three years—don't stop *now*." He added irritably, "Pick up that damn thing first. I can't reach it."

The almost sculptured head swept past him in a flash of flame, a long arm and slim fingers followed, the handkerchief was rescued and slipped in his breast pocket.

"Well?" he prompted. "You believe it. Say it. We've lived with it for so long it would be almost a relief. You think Maire O'Malley was my *grande passion* and that Shay's the result. Don't you?"

Her eyes scared him a little. "I don't know," she said tremulously. "I don't think I know—what I think, any more. That other merger, for instance—the one Myles wanted. You never told me." Dear heaven, Matthew thought, horror-struck, she was going to cry. He could never cope with weeping women. "Doug told Kate. It seems—I was wrong about Myles—too."

It was said so softly he doubted his ears. "*Too?*" he questioned sharply, and there was a pause. The neat head nodded. "A leopard can't change his spots," he warned. "You'd sew Paris up much more quickly without me. But of course we should really go on to Rome,"

Another pause. Then: "Why not?" Sheila responded. "We're not tied to time. Shay can hold the fort. We're— lucky to have him."

Johanna, tortured by fears that she had done wrong, was immensely relieved by the atmosphere at dinner. Matthew and Sheila far from being at each other's throats, seemed astonishingly friendly. Towards the end of the meal Sheila even said to her with a smile: "I think if we asked that doctor nicely he might let Doug have one outside visitor tomorrow if you'd like that, Jo?"

Johanna was giving eager assent when Kate, who had been called to the telephone, came back looking startled and almost bothered. "That was Maire. She's just had a call she thought we should know about it. From Geraldine Baldwin asking for a bed for the night."

"Geraldine! She's in London—going on to Paris," Sheila began.

164

"She's not then," Kate informed her in a tone that made no secret of her feelings. "She's in Donegal, just off the bus from Belfast, and waiting for a lift out here. Maire says she's flying back to London tomorrow. This is just to see Doug."

"For Pete's sake!" Matthew exclaimed. "We must be paying her too much!"

"Oh, Matt," Sheila deprecated, "it's natural she should come. They're practically engaged."

Johanna said nothing. Her mouth had suddenly dried.

As was only to be expected, when Sheila O'Malley put her visiting request to Douglas's doctor next morning, it was in favour of Geraldine.

"You understand, Jo? She has to be off again so soon."

Geraldine was operating on a skin-tight schedule. Her plane left Belfast at seven, so she would have to leave Carrickdoo immediately after lunch. Sheila was driving her in to the hospital around eleven o'clock.

"I think I'll go and see how Flann is," Johanna said.

"Do, darling," Kate agreed. She gave Johanna's face a searching glance. "It's disappointing, I'm very sorry. But I don't see what else Sheila could do."

Flann was actually wagging his tail, and Vincent O'Neill was full of details to give Douglas. She was trying to memorise them when a familiar white Mercedes drove up the veterinary surgeon's drive. The head, however, which leaned through the driver's window, was not titian but dark, the hair upswept. It looked like Geraldine's hair-style. It was.

"Hullo there!" she called chummily. "Hop in!"

"And don't look so horrified," she laughed as they reversed out on to the road. "I'm not planning to abduct you. All clear behind?"

All behind *was* clear, a lot clearer than in front. "I'm not looking horrified," Johanna said quickly. "Just surprised. I could have walked back."

"I don't doubt it," Geraldine returned still gaily. "But

165

I suffer from big-heartedness. Didn't you know? I wanted to see you," she explained as they drove. "About those designs. We've had a great time with them." It made it that much worse that her praise was unrestricted. Added to it were messages from Shay. "And they all want more," Geraldine concluded. "Not just for Young O'Malley but the trade ranges. We've got another British firm nibbling there. So all in all you've got a bright future and I thought you should know about it."

"It's terribly nice of you," Johanna felt wretched with self-condemnation. "I do appreciate it."

Somewhat surprisingly, the violet-blue eyes narrowed. "Ye-es, I felt sure you would. And that it would be a pity to spoil it."

"Spoil it?" A hot wave surged to Johanna's cheeks. She touched them nervously.

"Oh, even you can't be as innocent as all that," Geraldine sighed. "You'd be out on the street, girl, the O'Malleys wouldn't touch a thing of yours, *if they knew about you and Myles.*"

Had it been a hot wave? It was now an icy cold one. It went as far as Johanna's palms and further, down to the pit of her stomach. "Who told you?" The question was unnecessary. Only one person could have.

"Shay."

"But he promised. Oh, how could he!"

"Now keep your hair on," Geraldine said roundly. "He was flaked out. I really don't know how he kept vertical at all. He'd been on the go all day and at night there was this party, the kind where they don't ask if you want any more, they just keep filling your glass. Someone asked about you and he let it slip that you'd known Myles, just that, nothing more. I got the rest out of him in the taxi afterwards. He was so exhausted then that he didn't know whether he was coming or going." She said it calmly and unashamedly.

"But—why?" Johanna asked. There was a curious

emptiness inside her that made her, at the moment, only curious.

"*Why?*" It was Geraldine's turn to echo. She drew in to the side of the road and stopped. "Johanna, I'll level with you. I'm sorry about you and Myles. It must have been ghastly. But you can't have Douglas in lieu."

"Oh no!" Johanna gasped. "No. It was *never* that!" Her head was swimming. How could it be thought . . . she gestured hopelessly.

"A manner of speaking," Geraldine said coolly. "You *are* developing a thing about him, aren't you?"

"I—care for him, if that's what you're asking," Johanna acknowledged.

"Not asking, telling," Geraldine returned. "You're the girl who won't take hints. Look, I don't like this. You can take that or leave it, but I really don't. I hoped it wouldn't come to an ultimatum, but as I've said, hints got me nowhere."

"Hints?" Johanna echoed, mystified.

Geraldine laughed quite pleasantly. "We may as well be civilized about it, I suppose. I saw this coming, before you did, I think—that very first day in Mrs. O'Malley's office when you said you'd met Doug at the exhibition in London and wanted to help. I didn't exactly warm to the idea that you should be brought up here to the factory."

"That was *Shay*," Johanna said flatly. It seemed a disproportionate injustice that the whole campaign should have started because of a silly mistake. "I was talking about *Shay*. I thought *he* was Myles's brother."

"Well!" The little laugh came again. "If you don't get your facts right it's not my fault."

Now, I just want you back in England so that Doug and I can take up where we left off. I think he *has* got a bit of a thing about you at the moment, but he'll forget once he gets back to his work. By next year we'll probably be married. And, as you *are* fond of him, don't worry. I'll make him a very good wife."

The silence, probably quite a long one, was so full of turbulent thoughts that Johanna had no account of time. Damocles's sword she had always pictured dropping like a thunderbolt and splitting the world in two. Instead, it had inched down, almost gracefully, to its target. Every inch had been reasoned, undeniable, just. There was only one counter-blow and she knew how weak it was.

"You're very sure they'd mind?"

"Well, I don't think we need waste time on that one. They'd mind," Geraldine answered composedly. "Mrs. O'Malley, for instance, never saw Myles without the shining armour. She's refused all along even to consider that he might have been deceiving her. Mr. O'Malley's going to resent most of all that you didn't tell him the truth about yourself. That's his big crib since he can't get about, people don't tell him things or do things behind his back. However, with him you might just get away with it. He'll be the easiest. You'll have your work cut out with Doug. He was always dead sure you existed. He was on to that telephone call, you see, he said Shay should have got your name and address. He even thought of going to London and seeing if anyone at the college knew who you might be. You probably think it's quite unjust to blame you for the car crash, but Doug has a fetish about being responsible and straightforward. And of course he knows, none better, the repercussions it's had.

"So there it is," she said a few minutes later. "Entirely up to you."

It had taken only the few minutes to decide, or rather to pinpoint the final decision. All previous arguments against telling Doug were strengthened a hundredfold and, in addition, there was the new pain she would be inflicting on Sheila O'Malley. "Not peace but a sword," it said somewhere in the Bible. Johanna felt no words could have produced a better summing up.

"They mustn't know. So what do you want me to do?"

168

"You have your air ticket," Geraldine said simply. "I just want you to use it, tomorrow, as planned. Now listen carefully. I'm used to this sort of thing and I've got it all worked out."

Carrickdoo, one of a union of parishes, had its hours of service on a rota. To-day Morning Prayer had been at noon and Kate expressed disappointment that Johanna had not accompanied her. "Visitors are always a treat."

It took something to answer as though nothing had happened, particularly when Johanna had spent the time writing her a letter. A lamentably feeble one, she felt, as she sealed it. Kate would be dumbfounded, would never understand why she had suddenly felt it "better to stick to the original date for going home," would never understand, that is, until Douglas told her what was in the letter addressed to him, the hardest of all to write, the letter saying no.

He, according to Geraldine at lunch, was "marvellous". She herself had returned from the visit in almost theatrical high spirits.

For Johanna nothing had been forgotten. A factory car would wait for her outside Kate's gate at eight-fifteen tomorrow morning and take her to Donegal for the nine o'clock bus to Dublin. This would get in just before two and conveniently the bus station was also the pick-up point for the airport coach. Geraldine promised that she would herself pack and send on the belongings Johanna had left in Knockbeg. "And what about the kitten?"

But after a moment's thought Johanna had said no. Ken was part of the dream. It seemed he should stay that way. Someone could then bring him back to Kate, who after all had never wanted to part with him.

The schedule was water-tight; Geraldine had not been a secretary for nothing, and since Sheila and Matthew O'Malley, like Kate, took breakfast in bed it was quite easy for Johanna to slip away.

Fifteen hours later she was dragging her weary feet past the ticket barrier on Norwich station and her father's arm, blessedly strong and welcoming, had reached out and grabbed her.

When Geraldine arrived back in London on Sunday night Shay was not in the hotel. He had left her a note saying that he was with the Felgate-Winters but would see her at breakfast. The note added that seats had been taken for them both on a morning flight to Paris.

Falling into bed, tired and burdened, the Paris trip was not the thing on which she would have chosen to sleep, and next morning it seemed that Shay shared this view. First in the taxi and then in the coach his mood could only have been described as grumpy.

They reached the depature lounge to hear that the flight was delayed.

"All right, no need to snap my head off," Geraldine said resentfully, her suggestion that they should have coffee while waiting having been poorly received. "We're all in the same boat."

"I wish to heaven I was," Shay retorted.

"Of course, I forgot. You don't like flying, do you? Why, then?"

Shay said tetchily that the arrangements had been made by Mr. Felgate-Winter's secretary. "You shouldn't have been in Ireland, you should have been here looking after me."

On the plane he protested: "Good grief, not by the window. We don't want to look out," and when they were airborne after a perfect take-off he sat tensely staring in front of him.

"You know, what you need is a Scotch." She had slept badly and at the moment of waking it had all flooded in on her. She had thought: "I can't cope, not to-day," and then: "It's not fair", but if it were nothing else it was that. Douglas had always been fair. It was a far cry, that was all, from him to Shay.

He seemed apathetic about the Scotch, so she bought it for him. "Your mother is worried about you. She says you're being exploited. She wanted to have a go at them, but I stopped her."

"Thanks," Shay responded with a shudder.

"Just the same, it's true. You've had no leave. You should insist when we get back. Have some time with your mother before her term begins." She liked Maire O'Malley and it was a plea she knew would never otherwise be made.

"Come too?" Shay invited.

"You know we can't both be away together."

"Well, I'm away at the moment—unfortunately," he said with a yawn. "Where are you?"

Right, she'd said a daft thing, it was odd that her first reaction should have been that and not a straight no. Odd that at this of all moments she could bear even to contemplate Carrickdoo. But then it would be a different Carrickdoo, meals knocked up any old time, plates carried in and out to television set, fixing sunflower tiles in the kitchen. Those weekends had been fun. "What about Johanna?"

"What about her?" He seemed to be having difficulty with his yawns. "Not her fault. She tried. I just know." The black head went down on Geraldine's shoulder. Its owner—"out like a light", she thought incredulously— let an arm flop sideways across her.

She wished she could sleep herself, shutting out yesterday and Douglas's face when she'd put her head round his door. The light had died in it, quite slowly, quite silently. Hard on her heels Sheila had filled the gap, "Kate and Jo were dying to come, but the doctor said only one visitor and we knew you'd want to see Geraldine."

"Oh yes, yes, of course I do," Douglas had said instantly, stretching out his hand.

He always met you halfway. It was how it had all begun. "My mother tells me you've been wanting to see that show at the Gaiety. Would you like to come with me?" and Sheila's eager: "Well, did he ask you?" had left not the slightest doubt as to whose the idea had really been.

So kindly meant, and the invitation so much wanted, that she'd accepted with pleasure. But from the start Douglas had been honest. Would she just look on him as a stopgap for, though he enoyed her company "very much indeed," he was not thinking of marriage. And at the end of twelve months' regular dating he was still a pal, nothing more. Though until yesterday she had hoped. Yesterday when they were alone, he had said it, fairly and squarely: "I wanted to tell you, actually you're the first to know, I've asked Jo to marry me."

She could have said it in nine short words: "You know she was the girl Myles was meeting?" but she hadn't. *Not while he's ill, but she won't get away with it. I'll tell him later.*

Now, most curiously, she knew she never would. She had her hands full anyway—or was it more correct to say her arms. It was coming back to her that you should never administer spirits when people were strung up.

Shay's black head still lolled on her shoulder, his lips slightly parted showing the division in his front teeth, he had a child's tiny mole on his neck and when, embarrassed by the stewardess's smile, she tried to stir herself, a slim brown hand still in sleep tightened its hold upon her.

## CHAPTER FIFTEEN

"Look, Mum, if he's busy . . ." Johanna began for the third time. She was standing in front of the house waiting for her father to drive her into Great Yarmouth.

The purpose of the expedition was to vet a car which Johanna was buying to take her to and from the art school where term would shortly commence. Her father was financing the purchase, so he deserved a say in it, besides which he had a better ear for engines than his daughter. All the same he was being very tardy and these days the smallest thing seemed to make her irritable, almost ready to cry. Try as she might, it was hard to conceal, and she knew that even her mother's detachment was being strained to breaking point.

Dorothy Dykes had even started probing, a thing unheard of for her. She was probing now: "I've been thinking about that family you were with, darling. You say they're in the tweed business. Did they know Myles?"

The longest shot to date and Johanna flinched from it. Remarkably little had been said by either of her parents in the first week of her return and she herself had been, unfairly, the proverbial clam, even to side-tracking skilfully any mention of her employer's name.

Now she began to say: "They could have," and was interrupted almost startlingly by three large black and white birds zigzagging in flight to a telegraph wire.

"Oh, look!" Dorothy Dykes pointed. "Three for a wedding!"

"Do we still have all seven?" Johanna asked.

Her mother shook her head. "No. The person with the secret must have told it." It looked as though her eyes met Johanna's by accident, but Dorothy Dykes seldom did things that way.

It was no use, Johanna decided. They were her parents after all and the sense of their love and anxiety had never been greater than in the past fortnight. "Right, Mum, you win; they *were* Myles's people. That's why I wanted to help. But they didn't know we knew each other. There was no use stirring up the past."

"But, darling, I'd have thought . . ."

"*No*, Mum! It was best. And anyway, it's over now."

The silence that had followed her flight from Carrickdoo had been total. True, a week ago, her clothes and the other odds and ends she'd left in Knockbeg had arrived. Her

173

address, of course, was on record with the firm. But from Sheila, Matthew or Shay not a line. And from Douglas —nothing. Could she expect anything after that letter?

"My dear Douglas,

Forgive me, please, for not being brave enough to see you again. I've thought and thought and I feel sure this is best.

I will never forget my weeks in Ireland and your many kindnesses. Get well soon, and take care of yourself.

Jo."

Shay's letter addressed to Knockbeg had been longer and easier to write. Somehow it was like putting into words what she felt they had both known when he'd kissed her good-bye that night at Dun Laoghaire.

Disconcertingly, her mother was studying her face. Even more so was the question that came. "Then Douglas is—or was—Myles's brother. Is he like him?"

"No, not at all, Johanna replied. There remained an expectant silence. "He's quite a bit older," she went on hesitantly, "and not as tall, and his eyes are grey. He's a vet and terribly busy, you know how it is, but he was very kind when we did meet. He's kind to everybody. On Saturday afternoons the children for miles around bring him their animals to look at."

"He sounds nice," her mother commented.

"He is." Johanna was glad that at that moment her father appeared.

Johanna would have been content with the car, her father turned it down. He was more impressed with the next one they were shown but provokingly shook his head when the garage man offered them a trial run.

"Not just now, I'm afraid. We're pushed for time."

The Mini was left for further consideration and Johanna, finding herself being hustled back into their own car, felt justifiably annoyed: "What's the idea, Dad? Anyone would think we were catching a train."

"Not exactly, love, but you're getting warm," her father declared. "I've something to pick up at the station."

They bumped over the railway bridge and stopped. It was peaceful and empty-looking.

"Wonder if she's in?" Edward Dykes muttered.

A day in the season, Johanna thought, there would be no need to wonder. The station precincts would be black with holidaymakers streaming off the Liverpool Street or North of England trains, surging for taxis or the special buses that plied on Saturdays. And then it hit her. *Why was her father bothered?* They were not meeting a passenger.

"Dad?" She got no further.

"Quick! Out." Her father was spluttering. "She *is* in." He had opened his door.

Mystified, Johanna opened hers, ducked out, straightened still amazedly and felt the expression freeze on her face.

"Now. See anyone you know?" her father was demanding.

The station had cleared quickly since these days tickets were issued on the train, but in the No Man's Land between the platform and the Way Out a single chunky figure was standing between a suitcase and a covered basket.

They saw each other simultaneously. In her dreams—and almost every night since she'd come home this had happened—they'd rushed forward, both of them, with their arms out. Reality was somewhat different. Douglas sketched a wave and stooped to pick up his luggage. He walked briskly, she loitered. Thoughts flashed in—he looks marvellous, he's so brown, his face is fuller.

And then: "Hullo," said Douglas. "Nice to see you again." His eyes went past to her companion. "Mr. Dykes. Hope I'm not being a frightful nuisance." He gave to Edward Dykes's disclaimers his full attention. You would think, Johanna fretted, that he was a friend of her parents' rather than of herself. When? How? Why? Questions chased through her brain.

"Douglas! Are you better?"

"Oh yes," he said it cursorily, almost contemptuously. "And back on the job, as you can probably see." As she stared his eye went to the basket. "I think this is where you came in, isn't it?" he asked seriously. "One kitten, male, marmalade, immunized, abandoned by foster-parent."

Johanna scratched the basket lid and was answered by Ken's happy squeak.

It was still a dream to Johanna and one that was not proceeding according to plan. Her father was taking up far too much of the conversation and Douglas seemed perfectly content that it should be so. The visit itself was on a par with this—communication apparently between Douglas and her parents but not a word to her.

Other news came over supper. Flann was also back in residence. "Thanks to you and Vincent." The grey eyes softened and Johanna's heart missed a beat. It missed a few more when Douglas explained that while he had been tackling one intruder, the other had made to get away and Flann had jumped him. "Danes will often let a villain in and then not let him out." But in this case the villain had had a knife and a cosh. The moment when Douglas had gone to his dog's aid had been his own undoing. "Daft, of course. They keep rubbing that in. Heart is a commodity no cop can afford on duty." He added that since then his assailant had been apprehended and both men were now in custody awaiting trial. They were not tinkers. The tinkers had merely played the part of decoy, and even this could not be proved.

For the rest, Shay was in Carrickdoo at the moment, having some leave before next month when Matthew and Sheila were going on a joint business trip. Geraldine, he threw in as casually, had also gone to Carrickdoo.

While Johanna was struggling with all this, her mother looked down the table: "More coffee, Douglas? No?

Then you and Jo go inside to the television. Ted and I won't be long."

"By Jove, yes. That thing I like is just coming on." Her husband rose with alacrity and was frowned down. It was such an obvious frown that Johanna did not see how Douglas could have missed it. He had not.

"Now then, how long have we got?" he asked briskly in the sitting-room.

"How long for what?" she asked.

"For you to come to your senses—about marrying me." No pleading, no sign of doubt. More of Matthew O'Malley in Douglas than she'd realized. And in this new Douglas seemingly nothing of the man who had held her so tenderly that night on the shore.

"I—did," she said softly. "I thought and thought before I wrote that letter. There's nothing more to be said. Really there isn't."

"I think there is. A lot," Douglas returned, and sat forward squarely, his hands between his knees. "That's why I wrote to your father and asked his permission to call."

Johanna's mouth dropped open. "You did what?" A ripple of laughter followed, she couldn't help it. "I don't suppose he knew what to say. Poor old Dad!"

"He knew *exactly* what to say," Douglas replied with dignity. "As I would expect, having met him. He told me to come over and let him have a look at me."

"I don't believe it!"

"Well, I can't see much wrong with it," Douglas answered calmly. "It's exactly what I shall say myself when the time comes with our daughter."

"Our—daughter?" Johanna gasped. There was something about the new Douglas that was sending the blood coursing through her veins.

"Aye. Our daughter. With a face like a little pussy-cat just like her mother." He looked at her as though daring her to deny it, a cocky look and very young.

"No, please," said Johanna desperately. "Please don't go on. It's no. It's got to be no."

"Geraldine was afraid of this," Douglas remarked staggeringly. "She had a word with me when she got back from France. She thought she might have given you the wrong impression." The tone was dry. "If I had never met you, Jo, I still would never marry Geraldine. Sorry if that sounds crude. I have enjoyed her company and she's a tower of strength to my mother, but I'm not in love with her. There need be no conscience for either of us about Geraldine. She'll tell you that herself—now." In the little pause he suddenly looked impatient. "Don't be too hard on her, love. Most of us have silly things about people once in our lives."

"Jo, what is it?" Her silence had got through disturbingly. She saw the changed look in his eyes. "Is it—what I said just then about—silly things?"

She thought frantically. He had never been Geraldine's. To marry him would be robbing no one. And he still wanted her. And he was a man, not a boy. It was a man's way he had chosen—always—to-day most of all. And then the gladness ebbed. To marry him now without telling would mean a lifetime wondering whether Geraldine would keep silent. It was out of the question. And to tell him—no! He would not then want to marry her, but he might feel bound to. Besides, he was a man—a complete man—losing her would not crush him. He would get over it.

"I won't have it called a silly thing—ever," she chose her words carefully. "It was a beautiful thing, an enchanted dream, and I want to keep it that way."

The silence seemed endless.

"Oh, Douglas, why did you come?" she cried despairingly.

"It seems I've been wasting my time," Douglas said quietly, and got to his feet.

Another mother might have questioned, Dorothy

Dykes did not, neither when Douglas declined politely but very firmly to occupy her spare room, nor after her husband had driven him back to Great Yarmouth to get a bed for the night. She said merely: "You were right, darling. He is very nice," and went off to look out a basket for Ken to sleep in.

Getting to bed was one thing, getting to sleep another. Hours later Johanna was still awake. She had heard the car being driven into the yard and her father slam its door. She had heard him call out: "Nice fellow that. What did you think of him?" It was a one-sided eavesdropping since her mother's voice did not carry, but she must have asked if Douglas had got accommodation. "Easily. They're all emptying out this week," Edward Dykes boomed in reply, and gave the name of the hotel Douglas had picked. It was on Marine Parade, facing the sea. Johanna knew it. Not that that mattered. It might as well be in Timbuktoo. Resolutely she closed her eyes.

It was a dry morning, the sky high and a hard pale blue. From Britannia Pier, Marine Parade, her childhood's mecca, stretched before her with its flowers and grass plots, the glass Biergarten, the ballroom tower, the top of the helter-skelter in the Pleasure Beach. Douglas's hotel, white with smart touches of colour, was easily located. She parked and ran up its steps.

"Oh dear! Mr. O'Malley?" The receptionist shook her head. "I'm afraid you've just missed him. He checked out five minutes ago."

"Oh no!" Johanna exclaimed tragically. At least she must say good-bye properly.

" 'Fraid so," the receptionist was confirming when the hall porter stepped forward. "If you're looking for Mr. O'Malley, miss, he's got to come back for these."

No sight had ever been more joyful than Douglas's suitcase with the empty cat basket sitting on top.

"When he does, keep him. Don't let him go," Johanna babbled, and ran down the steps again.

Which way? South to the floral clock, north to the swimming pool and the greens, or straight ahead over the wide island-bisected roadway and the pinkish-grey promenade to the sea? Johanna plumped for the sea and went half-running over the grass and paving to the far edge of the promenade. At the jetty, running unpretentiously between the two pavilion-crowned piers, she halted, staring and knitting her brows.

Not one but two figures were walking down it, the one thick-set and purposeful, the other dot-like but valiantly keeping pace. It was Douglas, even from the back there could be no doubt about it; the small child heading off with him was an unexpected complication.

They walked towards her, Douglas breasting the breeze with his hands in his pockets and his tie fluttering, the child, squat, blackberry-like and, she thought, male, trotting alongside. The stride lengthened. Douglas was obviously not relishing being faced by a frantic parent or worse.

"Hullo. Still the Welfare Officer, I see?"

Douglas stopped as though transfixed. "Jo!" and then again: "*Jo*"

A momentary shyness sent her eyes away from the light in his.

"Who's your friend?" she asked.

"I wish I knew." He looked bothered. "Dropped from heaven. I turned round back there and there he was."

But as Johanna was arguing that they should all go in her father's car to the Police Station and Douglas objecting on the grounds that all child-abductors took them into cars, when the object of the discussion announced cheerfully: "I live along here," and pointed up a side road off the Parade.

They marched him along it and he selected a house with plastic flowers in the window. Seconds later he was being handed over to a weary-looking girl in advanced pregnancy. "You wait till your dad gets in, you won't half catch it," she said mechanically, and slapped the truant.

"Did you really not see him walking beside you?" Johanna asked curiously as they retraced their steps.

"No, I didn't," Douglas answered irritably. "The way I felt this morning I wouldn't have noticed the Loch Ness Monster."

"Was that my fault?" Johanna asked softly.

"No. Mine. Your answer couldn't have been straighter and I'd a right to accept it. No harm done. I hope, and no hard feelings?"

*Straighter* . . . it was all she heard and suddenly all she could think of. He thought her straight when for the past three months her whole life had been one tangled web of deceit. Sailing under false colours, winning gratitude she had no right to and, perhaps, even imprisoning him still further in the fatalism at which he had once hinted—the girls he'd liked never sticking to him. To that at least, *she had the key*.

"Doug," she said tremulously, "there's something I must tell you."

It had been so bright that it had seemed to make nonsense of the weathermen's promised "showers, thundery and prolonged in places" but in the last few minutes clouds had come from the west, licking over town and promenade. As Johanna spoke heavy drops of rain spattered the pavement.

"Quick! Get in the car!" Douglas seized her hand and they ran for it.

"Get much wet?" he enquired a minute or so later, shaking the drops off his lapels.

"Douglas . . ." Johanna faltered. Not for a million lost children or a million thunder showers would she be put off again.

She looked at Douglas sitting sideways, his arm

stretched along the seat. Behind him a living curtain of rain bounced into the gutter. His coat was open and his big chest filled every inch of his thin white shirt.

She caught her breath. "I'm the girl Myles was meeting."

The brows lifted fractionally. "Oh yes?"

"We were running away to Scotland to get married. We had to."

"*Had* to?"

"Yes, because I won't be twenty-one till next year and Dad thought we should wait."

"And Myles didn't?" She didn't answer. "What about you? Or weren't you consulted?" Douglas pursued in the same quiet tone. He had not moved a muscle and his eyes had never kept his thoughts more securely.

"I wanted what Myles wanted. I was—very fond of him." She paused.

"Go on."

She would almost have preferred to see what she'd dreaded for so long, the crimson of anger and recrimination, but his face was brown and cool and his voice very quiet. It was, she realized, the reaction of a man rather than a boy.

"I—let him down," she blurted. Again words failed her. She perched on the edge of the seat, her back against the steering wheel. A knee, round and childlike, touched Douglas's knee and because of what she was now saying she felt ashamed and jerked it away. She saw he noticed the gesture.

"Go on. You let him down. How?"

She coloured. "I . . ." and stopped.

"At a guess," Douglas remarked drily, "Myles said why wait for marriage? And you held out. Correct?"

She nodded.

"So he did the next best thing, sold you the Gretna Green routine?"

182

"No. I'm not quite such a fool as that. I knew there'd have to be some delay. About three weeks, I thought. I wasn't sure."

"Myles probably even less so." Again the tone was dry, almost indifferent. "Carry on."

"When the train got to Norwich I knew I couldn't go through with it. So I got out and telephoned. But it was too late. Shay told me."

"I see." A pause. The crunch, she thought, despairingly. He was going over it as so many times she had done herself. He would see her weak and vacillating as the instrument of his brother's death. And know for the first time the true nature of the girl he had wanted to marry. Sick with apprehension she waited, watching his face. It was unsmiling and serious.

"Somebody's got to say it, Jo. Have you taken leave of your senses?"

Incredulously it dawned that this was not outrage but impatience. As she gaped he went on: "It's out now—for the first time, I take it?" Still dumb, she nodded. "Then for pity's sake face it, look at it. All I can see is a girl getting her neck out of the noose in the nick of time. Or should I say remembering at the eleventh hour the sense she was born with?" He took his hand from the back of the seat and shook her knee rallyingly: "There, that didn't hurt too much, did it?" It was like the pat he gave to small animals after he had treated them. The hand was long and gentle, a true surgeon's hand.

"Oh, I don't know!" Recollecting herself, Johanna put a hand to her spinning head. "You—I—you don't even seem surprised."

"Surprised? No. Why should I be?" he returned briskly. "It's not news to me."

"Not n— but it must be. How . . ."

The hand came off her knee and covered her hands, both of them, strongly and warmly. "It's all right. I'm not a magician. I just had your call traced. The one you made from the callbox on Norwich Station." His eyes softened. "You forgot to hang up, you know, for about five minutes."

"I—I don't remember about the phone," Johanna admitted. "I don't remember much about anything. They said I fainted."

"It was a terrible shock. I'm sorry."

"I still don't see . . ."

"Well, I knew you were at the railway station in Norwich and you were so upset I knew you couldn't have been just anybody. And I knew Myles had a new girl-friend *and* I knew he'd spent a weekend with friends who lived outside Norwich. None of Myles's friends ever had names, so I couldn't identify you, and much as I wanted to, I couldn't hope to trace you if I went over."

Her heart missed a beat. This then had been no prevarication on Geraldine's part. He *had* contemplated a search.

"Why did you want to—trace me?" her voice was almost a whisper of fear.

"Well, if you must know," the young uneasy look that she had noticed once or twice before was back, "I was worried—in case you hadn't got your head out of the noose in time. And if I'd known then that you'd just done a faint I'd nearly have done one myself." Embarassment left him and he grinned.

For Johanna too came the first smile.

"So there I was letting my imagination run riot about a girl from Norwich or thereabouts, and then in you walked and told me where you'd come from and I felt this just couldn't be a coincidence, particularly when you turned out to know about design."

Suddenly she couldn't resist asking: "And how long was it before you decided I was—all right?"

Douglas's eyes seemed to have won again something of the blue of the Atlantic Ocean that night at Carrickdoo.

184

"Just about as long as it took me to fall in love with you."

"And—how long was that?" Johanna asked breathlessly.

"Oh, about five minutes," he answered casually. "Look, I thought we'd covered all that." Johanna found herself being drawn round into the circle of his arm. "What were the second thoughts for? Myles?"

She shook her head, stammering some of the things she'd meant to say to Myles on the telephone that fateful day. "No. That would never have worked. We wouldn't have lasted. Neither of us really loved enough for keeps."

"*I'll* last," Douglas promised engagingly. "Give me half a chance and I'll hang round your neck like an albatross even when I've lost all my feathers."

"Oh, charming, how romantic can you get?"

"It's a nice question," Douglas commented, his eyes roguish and brightly blue. His lips found hers and held them, his arms tightened their grip. She felt the rise and fall of his chest as once before she had felt it and been unnerved. It was different now, no secrets, no shadows, hardly even thought.

"Your parents?" she whispered.

"No, no, no." He seemed to know exactly what she was thinking. "My mother once, maybe. Not now. She's come to love you."

"Then—ask me again," Johanna commanded.

Douglas sat up, smoothed his hair and straightened his tie.

"Johanna, me darlin' wee girl, will you come and be 'herself'?" he asked.

"Ach, sure o'course I will, man dear," Johanna answered. "With a heart and a half."


THE END

**To our devoted Harlequin Readers:**

Here are twenty-four titles which have never been available from Simon & Schuster previously.

**Fill in handy coupon below and send off this page.**

# *Harlequin Romances*

## TITLES STILL IN PRINT

〜〜〜〜〜〜〜〜〜〜〜〜〜〜〜〜〜〜

Harlequin Books, Dept. Z

Simon & Schuster, Inc., 11 West 39th St.

New York, N.Y. 10018

☐ Please send me information about Harlequin Romance Subscribers Club.

Send me titles checked above. I enclose .50 per copy plus .15 per book for postage and handling.

Name ............................................

Address ............................................

City ............... State ............ Zip ............